About the author

Sourabh Mukherjee is the author of two psychological thriller novels – *The Colours of Passion* and *In the Shadows of Death*. He has also written three short story collections. *Romance Shorts*, a collection of dark-romance short stories, won the Golden Pen Award in the Monsoon Romance Contest (2014). The two-part *Beyond 22 Yards* on stories of love and crime from the world of cricket has garnered interesting reviews. The seven-part series *It's All About Love* is among all time best reads on premier mobile-reading platforms and online portals.

Sourabh's books have received accolades from readers, book critics and several dailies, magazines and websites from the mainstream national media. He has written columns for Sportskeeda and Yahoo! Sports.

An Electronics and Telecommunications Engineer from Jadavpur University, Kolkata in his day-job, Sourabh works in a senior leadership position in a global technology firm. Author of publications on emerging trends in business and technology as well as a textbook, Sourabh also sits in the Industry Advisory Boards of several premier educational institutions in India. He has spoken in technology summits in London and Las Vegas, as well as at events organized by Bengal Chamber of Commerce and Industry, Indian Institute of Foreign Trade, Symbiosis, Kolkata University, IISWBM, Techno India Group, University of Engineering & Management, etc.

Praise for the author and his works

"...a fast-paced potboiler which hooks you and keeps you glued to the plot from the very beginning."

– *The Times of India*

"With an almost Freudian understanding of how our childhood experiences influence our adult decisions, Sourabh's novel paints a stark picture of urban life in India."

– *The Hindu*

"...traverses the underbelly and upmarket suburbs of Kolkata... Mukherjee has the unerring eye of a master craftsman."

– *The Hindu*

"A heady concoction of thrill, mystery, psychology and humanity is what makes this book such an engrossing fare."

– *Business Standard* and *Punjab Tribune*

"Crisp, well-composed and in a good flow, there are no loose ends to irk your mind."

– *Yahoo News*

"...a page turner till the end with its fluid narrative infused with twists and revelations..."

– *Zee News*

"A psychological thriller in the true sense of the phrase..."

– *The Free Press Journal*

"...a good storyline with a meaningful plot, and of course flawless writing..."

– *Absolute India* tabloid

"Mukherjee has explored the materialistic, urban life, its turmoils and fragility of relationships."

– *World News Network*

"...a compelling assortment of stories with evocative themes, characters that are both intriguing and humane, and intense narratives at its core... Riveting and breath-taking short stories!"

– *The News Now*

the SINNERS

SOURABH MUKHERJEE

Srishti
PUBLISHERS & DISTRIBUTORS

Srishti Publishers & Distributors
Registered Office: N-16, C.R. Park
New Delhi – 110 019
Corporate Office: 212A, Peacock Lane
Shahpur Jat, New Delhi – 110 049
editorial@srishtipublishers.com

First published by
Srishti Publishers & Distributors in 2020

10 9 8 7 6 5 4 3 2 1

This is a work of fiction. The characters, places, organisations and events described in this book are either a work of the author's imagination or have been used fictitiously. Any resemblance to people, living or dead, places, events, communities or organisations is purely coincidental.

The author asserts the moral right to be identified as the author of this work.

Printed and bound in India

To my lovely wife Mou,
my partner in crime.

Prologue

The noise on the road was deafening, with cars honking and people shouting. Photographers and reporters jostled for space behind the police barricade, everyone vying for juicy titbits of the breaking news of the night. The cops, blinded by flashlights, were having a tough time managing the crowd. The drizzle did not help. There was frenzied clicking of all kinds of cameras, from the long-nosed ones of press photographers to the mobile cameras of curious onlookers. They stopped on their way and clicked away everything they laid their eyes on – the police vans, the unruly crowd on the street, the thirty-storeyed Prestige Apartments in Bandra – one of the plushest addresses in Mumbai, its entrance presently sealed off.

The television channels had already broken the news. The road was packed with vans with satellite dishes on their roofs, as journalists spoke animatedly into cameras, conjuring up all kinds of speculations. Death and the myriad possibilities around it always meant good business for news channels.

"...he was found inside his penthouse apartment, his wrist slashed..."

"...we don't know yet if he was alone when he died..."
"...forensic experts are inside his apartment..."

Vikram Oberoi, Vice President and Head of India Operations of NexGen Technologies, had been found dead inside his penthouse in the topmost floor of Prestige Apartments earlier that evening. The police had broken in and had found him in the living room, sprawled on the sofa, his wrist slashed, and the volume of the television inside the room turned up. An empty glass of whiskey and a bottle more than half empty were in front of him. The kitchen knife with blood all over its blade had been found lying on the carpet.

1

FOUR MONTHS AGO

Sonal Verma rushed to join the long queue in front of the bank of elevators on the ground floor of the imposing tower of NexGen Technologies inside Hi-Tech Park, the plush office complex in Andheri. Hi-Tech was the address of almost a dozen technology behemoths.

The men in the crowd stole glances at Sonal. With her hair tied back in a ponytail, silver hoops, glossy lips, a fitted purple shirt and black pants that accentuated her meticulously maintained curves, Sonal did attract her share of stares. Bored and groggy till a while back on a grim Monday morning, most of the men suddenly found a reason to cheer up, run their fingers through their hair, and suck in their tummies.

Sonal had joined NexGen a couple of months back. She had still not forgotten the horrors of the months before her taking up the job. She had left college with a degree in commerce, a pile of dog-eared books in her study, her beaming countenance in her convocation photograph and her dreams of making it big. It had not taken her long to almost give in to despair.

NexGen was the first company she had applied for, but had not heard back from them for quite a few months after leaving college. All she had were a few odd jobs, lecherous supervisors and an excuse of a salary. And then, her wait was finally over. She was offered a position at NexGen in the Administration department.

NexGen was *the* company to work for at the moment. Over the last seven years, NexGen had been steadily making its mark in the Indian market with state-of-the-art smartphones and smart gadgets at affordable prices. The bigger companies, including the large global players, were beginning to sit up and take notice.

Sonal had one more reason to look forward to Monday mornings. The dishy Vikram Oberoi, Vice President, who headed NexGen's operations in India. Vikram Oberoi was straight out of the pages of a Mills & Boon novel – in his late-thirties, six feet three, bright intelligent eyes, sharp nose, and a chiselled jaw-line. The unruly mop of hair added to his boyish charm.

"He is married," Prachi had told Sonal on her first day. Sonal had been fishing for information about the drop-dead handsome man, who had spoken to the new recruits for thirty drool-worthy minutes during the induction programme. "And the wife is quite a looker herself," Prachi had added, as if to set fire to the last vestiges of hope Sonal might have harboured. Prachi had been working as a Human Resources Executive in NexGen since the early days of the company and knew everyone.

"Oh, the best ones are always taken, aren't they?" Sonal had sounded justifiably disheartened.

"Well, truth be told," Prachi said, "Our man doesn't score high on commitment. Can't stay away from *temptations*, apparently. It won't take you long to figure him out." There! The resurgence of hope, however dim.

"Really?" Sonal had tried to sound incredulous. "With a gorgeous wife tucked away?"

"Yes, darling. Don't be fooled by the photographs of the lovely twosome from the office parties and the awards functions that decorate the walls of his office. There they don't seem to be able to keep their hands off each other. But, trust me, it's all a sham!"

"What do you mean? The wife is dumb enough not to know?" Sonal had sounded sceptical.

"Or, our man is too smart not to show!" Prachi had winked.

Sonal had a seat in the office along with her colleagues in the Administration block, not too far from Vikram's corner office with its glass walls. And while her eyes drifted in the direction of the boss' cabin far too often for correctness, it was not too long before Sonal could feel Vikram's eyes on her most of the time he was in his office, even as he took calls on the desk phone, or held meetings in his room.

Over the next one month, they progressed from occasionally chatting up in the pantry – Sonal invariably following Vikram with her coffee mug every time *he* needed to be caffeinated – to going together for lunch or a quick afternoon coffee in the cafeteria. Sonal did not care about tongues wagging over Vikram's friendship with the "hot, new intern in the Admin".

However, there was one person who was not happy with the boss' newfound amorous interest – Vikram's secretary Aarti Bansal.

2

Aarti was with Vikram in her one-bedroom flat. It had been raining for quite some time. The dirt washed away, street lights reflected on the wet roads. There were distant rumbles in the evening sky, sounding almost ominous. Very few cars sped down the empty road below. The room was half-lit by a single lamp on the study desk.

It was just the two of them inside the flat. They had returned a while back after dining at the Marriott in Juhu.

"I've been missing you for days, Vikram! I don't remember when we met last," Aarti's voice rose a couple of notches, the resentment in her tone pronounced. "And when we met today after weeks, we ended up fighting."

There were beads of sweat on Aarti's temples and above her lips. She was visibly tense. There was a bad taste in her mouth, not the kind you carry home after a dinner at the Marriott. Vikram tried to pull her closer, but Aarti freed herself and walked away towards the desk. She looked away, trying to hide the tears that were threatening to spill out.

"Aarti, listen—," Vikram tried to speak, but Aarti would not let him.

"I know what's going on, Vikram," Aarti turned around to face Vikram and continued, "I know your ways. I can't say I wasn't warned, but I didn't care to listen. I was such a fool! You're losing interest in me, Vikram. It's the new bitch in the office, isn't it?"

Vikram raised a hand. "Aarti, we don't need to be nasty here!"

"Am *I* being nasty, Vikram? It's you who didn't get tired talking about her all the time we were together this evening," Aarti's voice shook. "Everyone in the office is talking about the two of you. And it makes me sick! I get it. I'm now just the clingy, boring lover who nags and begs for your attention! Not very different from your wife, I guess."

"Aarti, come on! You're getting this all wrong!" Vikram hugged her tight, standing behind her. His lips moved up and down the sides of her neck. Aarti shivered, feeling his warm breath behind her ears. She had goose bumps all over. Her eyes were half-closed, her brow was creased, and her lips were parted. Aarti realized just how much she had missed that closeness for days! The conflict within her was driving her mad. A part of her wanted to throw the bastard out of her house that very moment. And a part of her wanted to melt in his arms then and there. Vikram was driving her mad and Aarti hated herself for letting him do that to her.

Aarti finally managed to get a grip on herself. She turned around and grabbed Vikram by the collar of his shirt. She whispered menacingly in his ears, "Vikram, I'll do anything to make sure you stay away from that bitch for good!"

She kissed him like a tigress famished; drawing the blood off his lips. She grabbed him by his hair as her probing tongue parted his lips, sliding into the wine-scented warmth of his mouth. Their tongues wrestled, and they disengaged only when both of them were gasping for breath.

"Vikram, I want to know why you're drifting away from me. You owe me a goddamned explanation, after we've been together for all these months!" Aarti clutched his collar, pulling him closer.

"Aarti, listen! You are imagining things," Vikram ran his fingers through Aarti's hair and spoke almost in whispers. "And do *not* put words in my mouth! What you are saying is a bunch of assumptions *you* are making. There's no way I can explain these."

"Vikram, I really wish I could believe you," Aarti said, lunging forward and kissing him again. "My life hasn't been the same since we started dating. Everyone in the office knows about us. I hate the way people look at me, the way they talk about us behind my back. I know you don't care, but it's not easy for me. Why don't you try to understand?"

"Are you complaining, Aarti? Why is it suddenly only *me*? I thought you and I are in this, together!"

"No, Vikram! I'm not complaining. And I know we are in this *together*! But I have a feeling you don't like me anymore, and that's what's making it very difficult for me." Tears welled up in her eyes.

"You are getting this all wrong, Aarti," Vikram repeated, pulling her closer and caressing her back.

"Vikram, I'm very confused. And I can't share this with anyone. Not even with the closest of my friends who had warned me about you. I didn't listen to anyone and went headlong into this, thinking it would just be a casual fling. It's probably just that for you. But, it has stopped being just a fling for me, Vikram. I don't know when this happened. But, when I see you with Sonal, I feel jealous. I can't stop thinking about the two of you. I wish I never landed up in this emotional space!"

Vikram kissed her and she responded, her body warming up.

Aarti pushed him into the couch and pounced on him, beginning to unbuckle his belt. As Vikram looked into her eyes, the madness he saw there made his heart skip a beat. And even though he had Aarti in his arms, her scent in his nose and her warmth wrapped all around him, it was Sonal that he was thinking of.

3

Vikram had dropped hints about meeting outside the office a few times, but Sonal had kept up the tease, refusing every time. Vikram loved that about a woman. It made the chase all the more exciting.

When Sonal finally agreed for a dinner date on a Friday, Vikram chose a restaurant at the opulent Marriott Renaissance, overlooking the serene Powai Lake. He had reserved a table in a corner and Sonal's heart skipped several beats when, after getting out of the elevator, Vikram held her by the small of her back and led her to the restaurant, his touch almost electric. The soft notes of the piano wafting in the air were soothing, the eating area mildly lit. Sonal saw red candles on the table. There were fresh rose buds in a vase placed on a spotless white table cover.

The questions came back to bother Sonal all over again. There was no doubt in Sonal's mind that Vikram was interested in a relationship with her. She did realize that indulging the advances of a married man at the workplace could jeopardise her career. But what about her own feelings? She had decided not to let her apprehensions get in her way. She had been biding her time over the last several weeks to prepare herself for that evening. And that moment had arrived, finally!

Her thoughts were interrupted by a waiter walking up to their table and lighting the red candle. Sonal looked at Vikram. He had been watching her.

"You seem lost," Vikram smiled. "Everything alright?"

"Yes – yes… everything's just fine," Sonal smiled. "Just that… all this feels like a dream!"

"A dream. That's what it is, Sonal. And we are living it right now," Vikram looked into her eyes, placing his hand on hers. His smile lighted up his face, his hand wrapped around Sonal's felt comfortably warm.

"Such a lovely place! Do you come here often?" Sonal asked him, looking around the restaurant, her eyes finally resting on the vast expanse of the Powai Lake.

"Not really. In fact, I don't usually go to restaurants when I'm alone. I go to bars where I drink, and munch whatever they have. The choices for food in a bar are usually limited, and I find that easier to deal with," Vikram laughed and then added, "But, this is a special evening." Sonal blushed.

The waiter came with the wine list and Vikram ordered a Chardonnay for both of them.

The waiter came back after a while. He showed Vikram the wine label, his face beaming as if he was showing him the picture of his only daughter. Vikram nodded in approval. The waiter unscrewed the cork with a pop, and poured a mouthful into a glass, which he offered to Sonal. Sonal smelled, shook and sipped the wine and nodded in approval like a connoisseur, which they both knew she was not. They stifled a laugh.

The waiter poured the drink in the wine glasses and another laid out plates with the starters. That was followed by the perfunctory "Enjoy your meal"-s and the waiters left.

After a few minutes of small talk about work, punctuated by moments of awkward silence, the words flowed between the two as did the exquisite Chardonnay. What Sonal observed, as they talked, was that Vikram never sounded guilty, never bitched about his wife, and never cared to cook up excuses to justify his ways, as most men tend to do when they are cheating on their wives.

As they were about to finish dessert, their conversation was interrupted by the buzz of Vikram's mobile phone. Sonal's heart skipped a beat. Was that his wife?

Sonal heard Vikram's side of the conversation.

"Hey chief, how's it going?"

"I'm actually in a restaurant right now, having dinner with a friend."

"Anything urgent?"

"Oh… can I call you back in... let me see... an hour maybe?"

"I will, Dev. Talk to you soon." Sonal realized it was Vikram's boss, the CEO of NexGen.

When Vikram finished the call, he looked at Sonal somewhat apologetically.

"Sonal, that was Dev. Looks like there's trouble! There's something he wants to discuss with me right now. Need to call him in an hour. I'm so sorry, but we have to make a dash." He was already gesturing towards the waiter.

❖

When the car stopped in front of Sonal's house, she turned towards Vikram and said, "Thanks for the lovely evening, Vikram. I'll always remember this."

Vikram was looking into her eyes. He leaned forward, and kissed her softly on her lips. "I will, too. This, and all the others to come, assuming I didn't bore you a lot, and that call from good old Dev hasn't blown my chance completely," he winked.

Sonal pushed Vikram back by his chest and smiled at him. "You didn't! Now stop planning our dates, and get back to work! Dev must be waiting for your call."

Vikram rolled his eyes. Sonal gave him a hurried peck on his cheek and got off the car, giggling like a teenager.

Vikram stayed back for a while, his eyes fixed on the seductive sway of Sonal's bottom under her little red dress. He ran his fingers through his hair, shook his head smiling to himself, and then started his car. As he drove towards his house, Vikram was sure like he had never been that Aarti Bansal was history.

4

Devesh Nair, or 'Dev' as he liked to be called, was the founder and CEO of NexGen. Dev had worked for Alpha Tech, one of the largest global manufacturers of consumer electronics for close to thirty years. Alpha was known for gadgets with features that set trends in the industry, but burnt a hole in the pocket of the average buyer.

Alpha's competitors, especially those from Asian countries, were catching up, manufacturing gadgets with comparable, and often better features at significantly lower prices. Dev fought every day with his bosses, trying to get their stamp of approval on his own innovative business plans that would increase market share. His plans, however, landed on deaf ears, as his bosses found them too risky.

One fine morning, seven years back, Dev gave up his job at Alpha, and put all his money into his dream project. Ashok

Pandey, Dev's friend from high school, who was an ardent believer in Dev's dreams, joined hands with him and threw in his lot with Dev. Ashok himself had no clue about technology, but was certain that Dev could never go wrong with his strategy. That's how NexGen was born.

In the next few years, NexGen invested heavily in research and innovation, and produced smart gadgets at highly affordable prices. Something Dev had always known was going to be the future of the industry.

NexGen was growing fast. Alpha was grappling with the dent in its market share in India. Dev was a happy man, much to the chagrin of Arun Sundaram, Dev's ex-boss and Head of India Operations at Alpha.

The last couple of quarters, however, had not been good enough for NexGen. Sales had declined for some of their products. Production costs had gone up. And, the market was suddenly very cautious about NexGen. Dev had been in the industry long enough to realize that he could not afford to remain a mute spectator, expecting his problems to take care of themselves.

Dev got a market survey done and when the results came in, he was able to put his finger on the exact areas that needed attention. He needed to talk to Vikram and take a few quick measures.

Dev picked up Vikram's call after the first ring. Vikram could figure out from Dev's tone that this was not going to be an easy conversation.

"Vikram, the quarterly results are out and I'm afraid we aren't looking as good as we used to *once upon a time*." Dev cut to the chase right away and Vikram did not miss the sarcasm.

"Are we declaring this week?" Vikram checked.

"We are. And we also need to make some announcements for our shareholders about what we're going to do about the poor show, right?"

"Yes, of course, Dev," Vikram tried to sound confident. He brought his hand to his nose. He could still smell Sonal.

"Vikram, the market is already saying our dream run is over and I don't want us to be seen sitting on our bum and not *doing* anything about it. I believe it's time we started thinking seriously about the merger with Quantum Technologies in Japan.

"Most importantly, the market survey results have come in and we've clearly not been able to make the kind of impact over the last couple of quarters as we've been doing till sometime back. The youngsters seem to be drifting away from us. What do you think we're going to do about *that*?" Dev sounded a bit helpless on the other side of the line. "Trends are changing very fast, Vikram, and looks like we have a lot of ground to cover!"

Vikram breathed easy. He had already made some progress on that one.

"Dev, I've been working on a plan to marry fashion with technology. We are drafting a proposal for partnership with Evita – "

"You mean the clothing and accessories line? What have *they* got to do with our technology?"

"Yes Dev, that's the company I'm talking about. We are in the process of drafting terms of engagement with Evita on a co-innovation program. I'll walk you through the plan tomorrow."

The line went quiet at the other end. Dev was thinking. He spoke after a while.

"I'm very curious to find out more. Let's discuss this tomorrow, Vikram."

Vikram looked at his watch. The conversation had been dragging on for too long. His throat was parched and he needed a drink. And, he was already undressing Sonal in his mind.

Dev continued on the other end of the line, "Let me warn you, Vikram. A couple more quarters like this one and we're all going to be screwed. You know and I know – we've invested far too much in research over the years. It's time to focus on returns now. And the competition is getting tougher by the minute. Alpha is fast catching up. The bastards are breathing on our neck."

"I understand, Dev. I will ask Aarti to set up a few meetings with Evita immediately. Let's see if we can expedite the collaboration discussions."

"That sounds good, Vikram. Get some sleep now. Let's talk about your plan for Evita tomorrow," Dev signed off. The line went dead at the other end.

Vikram looked at his watch and wondered if it would be okay to call Sonal so late.

5

"Dev, smart wearables! They are the next big thing!" With that one statement, Vikram captured Dev's undivided attention. "Always chase the next" – that was Dev's mantra. It was nine in the morning, and Dev had called Vikram as soon as he had stepped into office to better understand his plans for Evita.

"How would you describe that for the man on the street?" Dev reclined on his seat and asked.

"Well… think of a garment or an accessory that has embedded sensors, displays, and other forms of digital technology—"

"Cut out the jargon!" Dev raised a hand and stopped Vikram, "Let's get real here."

"Okay," Vikram shifted in his chair. "Let me give you examples from stuff that are already out there! Think of a cyclist wearing a jacket that looks just like a regular denim jacket, but has a touch-sensitive cuff, and the cyclist can touch that cuff and change music tracks, reject or answer calls, or access navigation information! Or, think of an accessory like a backpack, or a scarf, or a phone case that can change colours, by responding to body temperature, sunlight, wind, or simply by letting you select a colour of your choice! Or, you may want to put on a coat that looks just like the one you have on right now, but, there is intelligent heating technology hidden inside. It keeps you cosy inside that coat, depending on the temperature and humidity outside!"

"Wow!" Dev had already sat up straight. His eyes had widened. "So, this is 'wearable' technology that goes way beyond the fitness bands and smart watches everyone is wearing today, if I am getting you right!"

"You are spot on, Dev. And it's a huge opportunity for companies like us to catch on to."

"So, why isn't everyone doing this already?" Dev bent forward, his brow creased.

"Dev, a number of companies have actually tried and failed. And it's easy to figure out why. Buyers will pick up these products if they are stylish and trendy enough, and not just because of what they are capable of doing. These products need to *look* desirable. And honestly, Dev, fashion isn't something technology companies really understand," Vikram smiled and continued. "For example, we need to create an evening dress that's a beautiful piece of work which a lady would want to put on and go to a party, regardless of its technological value!"

"And are you saying that's where technology companies have failed?"

"Exactly! Until now, technology companies like us have owned the entire development process. Instead, what we really need is the marriage between a tech company like NexGen and a fashion house like Evita. Together, we will design and create products that will attract a hip buyer. We will design a beautiful accessory or clothing that a customer would desire. Otherwise, at the end of the day, all the tech features in the world will not sell if the customer simply doesn't want to *wear* the smart wearable!"

"All this sounds fantastic, Vikram! Now tell me what we're planning to do with Evita."

"Dev, the idea is to partner with Evita, and get their designers to work with our technology experts to produce fashionable smart wearables, just like the ones I talked about," Vikram continued to explain enthusiastically, "And then, we will go to the market together. We are planning fashion shows, advertisements in print, on television, on the Internet, the works. NexGen and Evita together will take the market by storm." Vikram paused briefly. "Oh, and I'm absolutely certain this will bring back a lot of our buyers, especially the millennials," he added with a smile.

"This sounds like a good idea, Vikram. Though I would be surprised if you tell me that no one has thought about this collaboration before. I have a feeling we already have competition here."

Vikram took some time to respond.

"Well, we do actually," he finally said. "I have information that Evita has been approached by a couple of our competitors with the same concept, Alpha, in particular. But, we have a partnership arrangement on the table which I am confident Evita can't refuse," Vikram sounded confident.

"Who's working on this?"

"I've got Ashwin working on the deal, Dev. We can't go wrong with this!" Vikram sounded smug.

"Well Vikram, we better get lucky with this. Mail me the proposal as soon as Ashwin and you are done with it. I'd like to go through it. We should be fine with making some concessions to make this partnership work, in the interest of gains in the long run."

"I'll do, Dev. And I'll block some time on your calendar tomorrow in the afternoon to walk you through our proposal," Vikram said. "Trust me Dev, we're putting together a proposal for Evita they simply can't refuse."

6

Agastya picked up the call from a private number after the third ring, taking his eyes off the monitor in front of him.

"Is this Agastya Bakshi?"

"Yes… who's this?"

"Agastya, my apologies for calling you late. I assure you this won't take too long. But, we need to talk in private. Where are you right now?" The male voice at the other end of the line sounded authoritative. Agastya could not recall having heard the voice earlier.

Agastya looked around the near-empty office and said, "I am at work, but we can talk. Not too many people around at this time of the night." His curiosity, by this time, was at its peak.

It was past eleven. It was the third time that week that Agastya had to work through the night. Hired a couple of years back, his work as an engineer in the Network and Systems Division of NexGen kept him rooted in front of computer screens through his days and very often, his nights. Agastya did not have much of a social life. A clumsy desk littered with pizza crumbs, empty cartons and soda cans, and a paunch growing at an alarming rate – that was what his life had been reduced to. But, he did not complain. Agastya loved his job.

"Great! Then let's talk business. I'm sorry I cannot disclose my name. I belong to a private investigation agency that's currently looking into the dealings of the company you are working for. There are reports of certain financial irregularities in the business."

Agastya sat up straight in his chair.

"Okay! But, what – what do you want from *me*?" Agastya asked tentatively. "I work in Network and Systems. I don't think you have the right number!"

"Agastya, I know who I am talking to," there was an almost imperceptible hint of annoyance in the voice of the man at the other end of the line. He went on, "We need access to the e-mail accounts of some of the top guys in your company to check their correspondences. And I've been told that you are the right man for the job."

Agastya took a sip of the cola that had already gone flat.

"Why – why *me*? You can speak to my Manager in the morning. He—"

The voice at the other end of the line did not let him finish.

"Agastya, this is a covert operation and we are a private agency. We cannot turn up at your office with an order to gain access to these accounts. Also, right now, we're not sure how many of the big guys are involved and in what ways. For all you know, your boss – the Systems Manager you are referring to – might as well be a party! Let's not forget that he has access to all records of transactions. We do not want anyone getting alert and tampering with the data we are looking for. We cannot risk exposure. It'll take us some time to complete the basic investigation. And I'd really appreciate your cooperation while we are at it. Once we have enough evidence at our disposal, we will make this official."

Agastya thought for a few minutes. The whole thing could be a hoax, for all it's worth!

"Look... how do I trust you?"

"I knew you were going to ask, Agastya. We'll be completely transparent with you. One of my agents will get in touch with you. You'll be working with her. I want you to hand over the details to her *in person*. This is for reasons of safety. And also, to make sure that you put faces to names. We want to win your trust and make sure that *you* are comfortable working with us because, as I said, this investigation isn't going to get over in a day. We'll need to work together for a while."

"I – I'll need to think this through. What's in it for me?"

"We'll most certainly compensate for your time and your cooperation. And I can assure you, you will have no reason to complain about the money. Don't worry about that," the voice sounded reassuring. Agastya did a quick mental calculation of the remaining EMIs for his new car. Almost at the same time, the full front-page advertisement of the upcoming apartment complex in South Mumbai flashed before his eyes.

The voice continued, "So I gather we're good to go here, right?"

Agastya mumbled an uncertain "Well…"

The voice did not seem to care.

"Thanks for your co-operation, Agastya. Ruchika will get in touch with you shortly. Have a good rest of the night at work." The man hung up.

Agastya looked disbelievingly at his phone. He wondered if he should call someone and discuss. The next moment, he decided against it. The man did sound like he meant business. And, in any case, Agastya was the one in charge. He was the one who had access to the data the agency was asking for. He was willing to give it a shot if the money was good. If, at any point in time, he had any reason to doubt the authenticity of the agency, he could always step back. Maybe even report the guy to appropriate authorities. He could always make an honest confession.

He put the phone down on his desk and went back to monitoring the data backup jobs. In a couple of minutes, his phone buzzed.

"Hey, this is Ruchika" – said the WhatsApp message.

"Hi", Agastya replied.

"My boss spoke to you a while ago."

"Yes."

"I thought I'd introduce myself. I'll be working with you."

Agastya added the number to his list of contacts. When the display picture showed up, his heart skipped several beats. He had not met anyone hotter than the girl staring back at him on the phone. Not that he had met too many girls, for that matter.

"Great to connect" – Agastya had assumed a friendlier tone already.

"Likewise, Agastya. Working late?"

"Yes. This is pretty much my schedule these days"

"Too bad" she typed, followed by a sad emoji.

"Hey, looks like I'm not the only one burning midnight oil… you are working too!"

"Yes…story of our lives, Agastya" – there was already a sense of camaraderie. And Agastya already had his pulse racing.

"Hey need to sign off now. I'll talk to you tomorrow. And let me know when we can meet. Chief gave you a task to complete, I believe"

"He did" Agastya added a smiling emoji, followed by *"I'll meet you with the data soon enough!"*

"Bye then… go back to your work… I won't hold you back anymore"

"I didn't complain" – Agastya winked.

"Hey, did you just try to flirt?" came Ruchika's reply, making Agastya wonder if it had been appropriate to flirt with her, just minutes after they had got introduced to each other on WhatsApp.

"Get back to work now," she said next, followed by a smile. The smile had the effect of reassuring Agastya. Ruchika followed up her smile with *"We'll talk tomorrow"*, which was followed by a *"Good night"*.

"It'll be fun working with you, Ruchika." Agastya stretched and thought aloud as he saw the girl going offline.

7

Ruchika was waiting restlessly in a room in The Orchid for her job that afternoon. She had called up her escort agency earlier in the day, saying she was too tired to work and would take the day off. She had done three nights in a row. Those nights had, of course, been memorable.

The first was with a business tycoon, among the richest in the country, who could not get it up with his wife, but was insatiable in bed with her. The next was with the captain of the winning cricket team in the T20 tournament, and she did not mind when some of the other well-hung boys joined the party. The tabloids and TV channels would be ready to pay her by lakhs, if she sold her story and the pictures from that wild night of team celebration, but she would never do that to those nice guys. And last night, she, along with a friend, was with this ageing Bollywood actor who liked it rough with much younger girls.

The job that afternoon was for her new-found patron, who was not willing to go through the agency, and preferred to do business directly with her. She had been promised a handsome remuneration. That way, she would not even have to part with the agency's commission. She could indeed afford to call in sick when she chose to, because the agency could not afford to lose her, come what may, thanks to her loyal celebrity clients spread all over Mumbai.

She checked her watch impatiently as she took another sip of the Merlot. It was for the first time that she had been handed a script for her job and asked to 'get close' to a client on WhatsApp and win his 'trust' over a few days before the job. And she thought that she had done her job perfectly.

There was a hesitant knock on the door. She put the wine glass down and stood up. She walked to the door, tottering slightly.

That, indeed, was the man she had been waiting for.

"Ruchika?" Agastya asked, ogling the girl in a light summer dress that ended above her knees, thin straps, plunging neckline showing ample cleavage. Over the last week, Agastya had progressed from acquaintance to friendship and finally, especially after a few drunk texts on Friday night, to intimacy with Ruchika, who had only been too happy to reciprocate. She had said that, she had a job that kept her busy almost round the clock through the year, leaving her with very little time to socialize. That had only enhanced the sense of solidarity between them.

"Oh hi, Agastya! So good to see you, finally! Do you want to check my ID?" she smiled, raising an eyebrow.

"Oh, come on!" Of everything she had to offer, her ID was the last thing Agastya wanted to see. "Don't embarrass me!"

Ruchika walked into the suite with an exaggerated swing of her hips, with Agastya following her like a puppy. She picked up her purse and fished out a badge.

"Well, you know what, sweety? I'm 'bound by duty' to show you my ID," Ruchika flashed a card in front of Agastya's lustful eyes. He barely looked at the card. She put the card back in her purse, and passed her arms around his neck. She inched closer and kissed him on his lips, pressing herself on him. "Now, show me if you are as good in real as you were in your texts," Ruchika purred in his ears.

Agastya had been in a dilemma over the 'assignment', even after planning their rendezvous in the hotel room. But feeling her in his arms now, in the solitude of the room, turned him on in a jiffy, and swept away the last shreds of doubt. Especially after the girl had shown him an ID. And, in any case, he was smart enough to find a way to cover his tracks in case something went wrong, he reminded himself once again.

As they sank into the sofa, she finished what remained of the Merlot in one long swig.

"I – I got the information your boss wanted me to—" Agastya's hand moved to the pocket of his jeans.

"Can we please not jump into business?" she looked into Agastya's eyes and placed a finger on his lips. Agastya read unabashed desire in her eyes. "What has developed between you and me over the last few days is far more important to me right now than what 'the boss' wants us to do," Ruchika whispered huskily into Agastya's ear, biting his earlobe, the fire in her breath searing.

Not quite in the mood for small talk apparently, she switched off her phone and inched closer to Agastya. She leaned onto him and felt the warmth of his body and his arm around her, first hesitant and then tighter and more confident.

Lightning danced across the dark sky outside as the untimely rain pelted against the glass windows of the hotel room, drowning out all other sounds. As she closed her eyes and parted her lips, she felt Agastya lower the strap off her left shoulder, his hand raising the short summer dress up her smooth thighs.

Ruchika was still in bed, the spotless white sheet pulled up to her chest, showing off her bare shoulders and her hair spread across the pillow tucked clumsily under her head, her body still glistening with a sheen of sweat, her clothes strewn on the carpet. Her eyes were fixed on Agastya. She was still wondering if the guy had ever been with a woman before! That would surely go down as the lousiest sex she had ever had. She wondered if she would have to have sex with him again. Then, she quickly reminded herself of the money. That calmed her down, somewhat.

Agastya stood at the foot of the bed with his back to her, zipping up and then buckling his brown leather belt. When he was done, he turned around. He walked up to her and his paunch jiggled. He bent down and kissed her on the forehead.

"I've got to go back to work, honey," he made a sad face. "This has everything you'll need to snoop into the accounts of all the guys you listed out." He handed her a pen drive and asked in the same breath, "When are we meeting next?"

"Whenever *you* find the time, sweetheart," she raised herself on her elbows, the sheet slipping off her shoulders, offering him an eyeful of her bare breasts, and kissed him on his lips. "I'm so happy we met!"

As he stepped out of the hotel room, Agastya fist-pumped into the air. He could not believe this was happening to him for real!

After Agastya had left, Ruchika switched on her phone and dialled a number.

"I've got everything you wanted," she spoke into the phone and ended the call.

8

Ashwin Saxena did not want to be late for work on that particular morning. It was around half past seven when he stepped into the shower. He made mental calculations. He would have to shave, dress, and get some breakfast in the next fifteen minutes if he were to reach office by nine-thirty.

Ashwin was the Sales and Marketing Director at NexGen. Ashwin had an easy charm, spoke eloquently and was known for his sharp power-dressing. More importantly, he was an expert in building business relationships. He did not have too many failures in his resume, and in a career spanning close to fifteen years, Ashwin built relationships with partners and clients that were strong enough to survive even the rare failures, which, most often, were for reasons beyond his control.

Ashwin and Vikram had not just grown together in NexGen, but they also shared a personal bond that went back several years.

They were from the same management school in Mumbai, and at different points in time through college, dated the same girl, Manvi. Manvi went on to marry Vikram.

By the time Manvi and Vikram got married, Ashwin had taken up a job in Delhi. There, he fell head over heels in love with Ashiya, who lived next door. When Ashiya's conservative parents opposed their marriage and her brothers threatened Ashwin with dire consequences, the two ran away from Delhi and took refuge in Vikram's house in Mumbai. Manvi and Ashiya became fast friends in those few months. Vikram referred Ashwin to Dev, who had been looking for 'sharp boys' for NexGen. It was not long before Ashwin came on board.

Ashwin had been eyeing the position of the Head of India Operations, but Vikram had beaten him to it. Ashwin held his grudge but continued to give his best to his work because, for him, failure was never an option. However, he had come to realize over time that, his success would ultimately translate into Vikram's success, fuelling Vikram's growth from strength to strength. And that did not always make him very happy. Evita's decision on the partnership proposal he had drafted along with Vikram was expected that morning.

"Ashwin, where are you?"

He could hear Ashiya calling from the bedroom. He popped his head out of the shower.

"In the shower, honey!"

Ashiya said something, but Ashwin could not hear her above the noise of the shower spray. He stepped out of the shower, wrapped a towel around himself, and asked, "What is it, Ashiya?"

"I wanted to check if can you drop Nusrat to school today."

Ashwin knew Ashiya had an appointment with the gynaecologist that morning, and had agreed to drop their daughter to school on the way. He wondered what had changed.

"Sorry, I can't today, Ashiya. Why, I thought you said you were going to drop her to school?" Ashwin asked as he lathered his face and started shaving. The clock on the bathroom sink already said seven-forty.

Ashiya came into the room as soon as Ashwin stepped out of the bathroom. She was holding the bowl of cereals she had been feeding the kid. Ashwin noticed once again, how beautiful his wife looked in the morning, fresh out of bed. Much better than she did when she put on make-up.

"I know, baby. But the clinic called. They are pushing all appointments this morning up by an hour, and I'll be cutting it very fine if I have to drop her to school on my way," she ran her fingers through Nusrat's messy curls. Their daughter was already dressed for school.

"Ashiya, I won't be able to, today. I'm so sorry," Ashwin had finished dressing and rushed to the kitchen to get himself a cup of coffee. He picked up a couple of oatmeal cookies.

"Please, Ashwin?"

"Ashiya, not today. I *have* to be at work by nine-thirty this morning."

"Okay, alright! Then, I'll leave right away, and drop her on the way," Ashiya pouted and went to get dressed.

A moment later, as he finished his coffee, Ashwin heard his wife call out to their daughter, "Okay Nusrat, let's go! Put your shoes on!"

Ashwin checked his watch as he picked up his car key. Seven-fifty. Not too bad.

Ashiya came back to him.

"Ashwin, don't worry. I'll manage. Sorry I was being a bit whiny." She smiled.

Ashwin kissed her on the forehead. "I'm so sorry, baby. Just a busy morning. I promise I'll make it up to you."

"Isn't today the big day? Evita is announcing, right?"

Ashwin was tying his shoe-laces.

"Yes, they are."

"You know you're going to make it, don't you?"

Ashwin smiled dryly. "Does it really matter?"

"What do you mean?" Ashiya looked surprised.

"NexGen takes *my* success for granted. It'll only add another feather to Vikram's cap," Ashwin stood up and headed for the door.

Ashiya kept looking at Ashwin's receding figure. She wondered what it was like not to be elated with success! That was not the Ashwin she had always known. Something had changed.

Big day indeed. For NexGen. For Ashwin.

More importantly, for Vikram.

9

Ashwin's office was on the twentieth floor. He had been hoping for a few years now to move up to the twenty-first.

He stepped out of the elevator at nine-forty, and walked briskly towards his room, swearing under his breath, angry with himself that he was late. The communication from Evita must have come in by now.

As soon as he was in, he powered on his laptop. It seemed to be taking forever to fire up and then connect to the network. When it finally did, Ashwin sat up straight and opened his office-mail.

There was already a pile of e-mails in his inbox. He ran through the names of their senders till he reached the mail from Adi Juneja, Alliance Director at Evita. He clicked the mail open.

The mail also had Vikram as a recipient. Ashwin read through the contents of the mail hurriedly.

Adi Juneja had conveyed his sincere apologies. Evita had decided to enter into partnership with another technology company.

Ashwin wheeled his chair back from his desk

He closed his eyes and ran his fingers through his hair, letting the news sink in.

Ashwin heard his phone ring. It was Vikram. He must have read the mail by now, too.

It was a blow for NexGen. For him.

Most importantly, for Vikram.

10

As Ashwin made his way towards Vikram's room, he could not help stealing a glance at Sonal, the events of the morning notwithstanding.

Sonal's rise in NexGen in an unusually short time had got tongues wagging in the office. She was being seen everywhere. She was organizing important meetings. She was making travel arrangements when the topmost honchos of the firm went on business trips. She was in teams organizing marketing events and product launches. Everyone in the office had come to realize that Vikram had the hots for Sonal and that, he had clearly ended his relationship with his secretary Aarti.

"Good morning, Sonal," Ashwin allowed himself a brief halt at her desk before entering Vikram's room, "Looking gorgeous, as always!"

The colour rose to Sonal's cheeks.

"Thanks, Ashwin. You have an early meeting with Vikram?"

"I do," Ashwin muttered, conscious all over again of the circumstances of the meeting.

Sonal looked at Vikram's office and whispered back, "I can see he is rather upset this morning."

"Tell me about it! This is not going to be easy…"

"My wishes and prayers are with you," Sonal laughed.

"Need all of it, Sonal," Ashwin checked his watch and sprinted to Vikram's office.

Vikram was pacing up and down his room, his arms folded behind him.

"This doesn't make any goddamned sense, Ashwin!" he thumped his desk. "You know what this means for us, right?"

"I don't get it myself, Vikram," Ashwin ran his fingers through his hair.

It was no wonder, given Ashwin's impeccable track record, that Vikram had entrusted him with the Evita assignment. The last time he had met Ashwin, Vikram had come out of that meeting feeling confident that NexGen was making steady progress.

"None of us had seen it coming, Ashwin!" Vikram thumped his desk again. "Do we know who the 'other qualified technology company' is?"

"It's Alpha, Vikram," Ashwin said. "There were two companies in Evita's shortlist – Alpha and us."

Ashwin had swung into action immediately after reading the mail from Adi, and had got in touch with some of his contacts in Evita. He had been investing in that relationship for several months now, and had made a few friends at Evita. He now filled Vikram in with everything he knew.

Apparently, Ashwin's friends in Evita could not build a convincing case in favour of NexGen when the Board members met the day before to decide on who would be a partner for launching their line of smart wearables. The deal had gone to Alpha.

"This is what I don't get," one of his friends at Evita had told Ashwin a few minutes back. "The proposal Alpha submitted looks every bit like yours! The only differences were that, they offered to share a marginally higher percentage of the initial investment and offered us a higher profit share. And they walked away with the partnership. In fact, we all joked about great brains thinking alike! Jokes apart, the similarities did look weird to all of us."Ashwin had found it difficult to believe what he had just heard. "It seemed as if someone had actually read every word of your proposal," the man at the other end of the line had added before ending the call.

"Vikram, the terms of engagement we had put down in that proposal were unique," Ashwin was now trying to explain, "It's very unlikely that Alpha would come up with exactly the same provisions unless—"

"Unless?" Vikram stopped in his tracks and turned towards Ashwin.

"Unless Alpha actually read our proposal. Unless someone from NexGen leaked the proposal out," Ashwin was direct.

"What the fuck do you mean?" Vikram looked at Ashwin long and hard and then shouted, "Are you out of your mind? Are you suggesting Dev or me—?"

"I didn't say that, Vikram!" Ashwin interjected.

"Then who else, Ashwin?" Vikram shouted. "The only persons who've ever got to see that proposal were Dev, you and I. We've never taken print-outs. We've exchanged drafts through secure company e-mails. And I don't remember any of our e-mail accounts hacked into for as long as I can remember. So how can the goddamn thing get out of this office and into the hands of those bastards at Alpha?"

"I... I have no idea, Vikram...but there can be no other explanation," Ashwin's tone gave away his reluctance to abandon his theory. He turned around and headed towards the door of Vikram's cabin. "I will keep checking with Evita. I'll let you know if anything else comes up." Which, both of them knew, was unlikely in the near future.

Ashwin left the room.

Vikram kept looking at the grey overcast sky. Dev would be calling any time now. His mind raced. He tried to remember if anyone other than Dev, Ashwin and himself had been involved in the discussions with Evita. He could not remember anyone.

This made no sense – no sense at all!

Vikram reached for his desk phone and dialled Agastya's number.

11

"Agastya, good morning."

"Good morning, sir," Agastya looked at Vikram's name and number on the display of his Cisco phone.

"Busy?" Vikram asked.

"Well… the same old routine, sir. Nothing unusual."

"Can you please come down to my cabin for a few minutes?"

Agastya assumed at first that Vikram must have run into a problem with his laptop or his network connection. He looked at the last slice of the pizza sitting on his desk and wondered if he should ask one of the other boys to walk down to Vikram's cabin. He decided against it when he realized Vikram's voice hinted at something more urgent than a broken link or a faulty laptop key.

"Be there in a minute, sir."

Agastya pushed his chair back, stood up and stretched with a groan, brushed the pizza crumbs off his tee and headed for Vikram's cabin.

❖

"Agastya, how secure is our company network?"

That was the last question Agastya had expected.

"It is… it is quite secure, sir," he muttered.

"Quite?" Vikram raised an eyebrow.

"I mean it's *very* secure, sir," Agastya corrected himself. "Why do you ask?" he looked puzzled.

"Tell me more about it," Vikram did not answer him.

"Well, we have a firewall in place. The antivirus, anti-spyware, anti-malware software is updated regularly. We have an Intrusion Detection System in place to figure out if someone is making an unauthorized access from outside. We also have security specialists carry out regular audits. They have always reported one hundred percent compliance, sir," Agastya rattled off.

"I see. Agastya, has there been a breach in the recent past? And I want absolute honesty here."

"No… no, Sir. I would have most certainly informed you, sir, had there been one…"

"Hmmm… you may go now, Agastya. Thanks," Vikram swivelled back in his chair to face his laptop screen.

Agastya headed for the door to Vikram's cabin and then suddenly stopped in his tracks. He turned towards Vikram and said, "Sir, you do know that as per company policy, we do monitor emails of our staff. And also the websites they visit while they are at work, right?"

Vikram looked up from the laptop screen, "Yes, I do, Agastya. But that's for our own monitoring. I don't expect anyone from outside to have access to company emails – our communications with partners and clients, for example. Am I right?"

"Yes… yes, sir," Agastya confirmed.

As Agastya stepped out of Vikram's room, he replayed the conversation in his mind. What was *that* about? He wondered if Vikram had found out anything about his nexus with the investigating agency. The first payment from the agency had reached his bank the day before. Should he exercise caution and step back? Agastya took out his phone and dialled Ruchika's number.

12

It had been a long day for Dev. He had been holed up in a conference room all day with Vikram and Ashwin, discussing how the Evita proposal might have been leaked out of the office. And more importantly, what should their strategy be going ahead.

By the time the day ended, he was craving for a drink. Once out of that discussion, he had headed straight for Ecstasy, which was his favourite watering hole in South Mumbai.

No sooner had he perched himself at the bar, loosened his tie and ordered a large Glenfiddich on the rocks than his eyes went to a boisterous lot, sitting not very far away from him. And he immediately recognized Arun Sundaram, his ex-boss and the Head of India Operations of Alpha Tech. Dev wondered if the team had gathered there to celebrate the Evita success.

Dev took a long swig of his drink and cursed Arun under his breath. In spite of himself, his eyes went back to the Alpha gang and to Arun in particular, who looked ruddy and beaming. And their eyes met.

Dev could not have said how long they kept staring at each other, but a stream of memories passed through his mind while they did. Dev remembered his days in Alpha and how working with Arun in his last few years in the company was nothing short of a nightmare. Peers once upon a time, Arun had raced ahead of him to become his boss, the means not entirely above board. Once he settled down in his position of authority, Arun started undermining Dev's ideas, calling them risky, impractical and immature. Dev's ideas, Arun said, reeked of Dev's 'complete ignorance of business realities and his theoretical mindset'. Everyone in the company knew who, between the two of them, was more practical and mature and that, it was Arun's own insecurity talking.

Coming out of his painful reverie, Dev drained his glass and ordered his second. He looked away from Arun. Arun smiled at him and raised his glass with a smirk. Dev realized at once that he should have seen it coming. In a flash, the hatred Dev had been carrying in his heart for several years raised its ugly head. Arun turned to his cronies, whispered something, and then, got off the bar stool, heading in the direction of Dev.

"Hey," Arun shouted, "Look who's here! It's Dev! *The god* himself!" Dev was not surprised at this unforeseen taunt. Words like 'decency' and 'diplomacy' had never existed in Arun's dictionary.

"Hello Arun," he raised his glass.

"Not a great week for you, is it?" Arun's tone of mock sympathy was not lost on Dev.

"I guess that's what business is all about," Dev tried to get out of the conversation. "You win some, you lose some." He forced a smile, stepping down from the bar stool already.

"Well… talking of winning, when was the last time you won *anything*?" Arun laughed, his whole body shaking, spilling his drink.

"Arun, I forgot to congratulate you on Evita. But, I can at least take pride in my honesty," Dev smiled disarmingly, as he passed on his credit card to the bartender. "I don't find it particularly exciting to win deals on stolen business proposals."

"What gives you *that* idea?" Arun put his glass down with a thud, spilling more drink. Dev was happy his words had managed to irk him.

"Common knowledge in my team," Dev smiled, looking into Arun's eyes.

"By your 'team', you mean Vikram? Mr Casanova?" Arun's face was red. "And talking of honesty, doesn't sound great coming from someone who set up his own company with ideas he had stolen from Alpha!"

Dev inched closer and stood within an arm's length from Arun. Their eyes bored into each other, their fists balled. Arun had poked a festering wound.

"Arun, you know as well as I do, that it was *you* who never let *my* ideas become *Alpha's* ideas. You had no value for them… and when I set up my own shop, those very same ideas took away a third of your customers!"

Dev was aware that a crowd had gathered around them. He gently pushed Arun to a side and made his way towards the exit. Arun regained his balance and picked up his glass, shouting at Dev, "Let's see how far your *ideas* take you! It's the beginning of your end, Dev!" He paused briefly and went on, "And your blind trust in your team is going to cost you dearly, my friend!"

Dev stopped in his tracks for a split second and reflected on what Arun, in his blind rage and drunken stupor, had just said. There was a furrow between his brows as he stepped out.

Maybe the idiot, for once, made sense.

13

Standing at the far corner of the Poison bar, a girl whispered into her phone, "I got him... Vikram's right here."

She ended the call and started walking towards Vikram, loud music thumping inside the club, revellers on the dance floor soaking in the blue haze.

Vikram had to raise his voice to be heard above the din at the bar, "A Macallan with three ice cubes." It was just what he needed at the end of a long, hard day.

He had spent the entire day discussing the Evita disaster with Dev and Ashwin. The discussions had not got them anywhere. They had come to accept among the three of them that information about the proposal had certainly been leaked out. But, none of them could figure out how. Vikram had walked out of his office an hour back and headed straight for Poison.

No sooner had the drink arrived than the girl walked up to the bar and stood next to Vikram.

She was wearing a snug off-shoulder top that accentuated her curves. Her hair was open, and it cascaded down to partially cover her breasts. She had big dark eyes, the lids somewhat droopy, and full moist lips. Her musky scent wafted in. Just as Vikram was about to take a sip of his drink, the girl turned to face him.

"Hey, I'm Kaamna. Are you alone?" she looked into Vikram's eyes.

"I am," Vikram replied with a smile.

"I'm looking for company myself," Kaamna said. "I won't refuse if you offer me a drink," she added with a suggestive wink.

"That was fast!" Vikram said with a smile. "So, what's your poison?"

"Whatever you're having," she said.

As he bent over the bar to call for the bartender, Vikram became acutely conscious of her supple yet firm breasts pressed against his upper arm. He stole a glance at the girl. Her bare neck and shoulders looked fetching. He felt the first stirrings of raw, unbridled desire coursing through his veins.

An hour flew by as they chatted, the casual conversation accompanied by meaningful touches. By their third drink, the girl had dragged Vikram to the dance floor and soon, the two were dancing very close. Kaamna pressed herself against Vikram, and writhed all over him in tune with a raunchy number. Vikram's hands got busy, as he drew her closer into his arms, her provocative moves turning him on insane.

Ever since Sonal had come into his life, Vikram had not had the need to indulge in the pick-up game. But it was Sonal's birthday, and she had wanted to spend the day with her parents. Vikram had been making elaborate plans, but his plans would now have to wait. Vikram was in dire need of his 'fix'. Also, thanks to this girl, for the first time since morning, he was feeling alive and rejuvenated.

He raised his voice above the music and shouted into her ear, "Want to go someplace quiet?"

14

As they made their way to Vikram's penthouse in the top floor of Prestige Apartments, he could not keep his hands off the girl. He kissed her roughly, caressing her all over.

"Baby, I'm so hot for you," Kaamna whispered in Vikram's ear, sinking her teeth into his earlobe. His tongue played with hers, even as the familiar "ding" of the elevator announced that they had reached their floor. Vikram barely managed to fish out the keys to his apartment.

He shut the heavy door behind them. He could feel her breathing hard, beads of sweat shining on the tip of her nose and above her lips, on her temples, in her cleavage. As he pulled her close, their moans and the rustle of clothes were the only sounds in the otherwise quiet room.

The sensuous aroma of her body was driving Vikram wild. He yanked off her top in one swift motion and cupped her firm yet supple breasts over her flimsy bra.

"Give me a minute, sweetheart. I need to go to the loo… too many drinks," Kaamna looked into Vikram's eyes and made a sorry face.

"Don't keep me waiting too long," Vikram freed her reluctantly and took off his shirt, as Kaamna threw her heels off and tottered towards the washroom.

No sooner had Kaamna come out of the washroom than Vikram scooped her up and threw her on the couch. As she lay on her back on the couch, Vikram got down on his knees on the carpet, showering smouldering kisses up her bare leg. Her pulse raced, and throaty moans escaped her lips as she squirmed under his touch. She began to remove her skirt.

When Vikram had dozed off on the couch, completely spent, Kaamna walked back to the washroom and picked up the camera she had turned on and positioned behind the slightly ajar door of a toilet-cabinet facing the couch. While stepping out of the toilet, Kaamna had made sure that the toilet door was left open while Vikram devoured her on the couch.

She transferred the camera to her clutch and walked out of the room. As she stepped into the elevator, she made a call.

"We made it! You'd love the show," she chuckled.

The line went dead at the other end. Kaamna flipped her phone shut as she walked out of the elevator into the balmy night.

15

Vikram walked into a quiet house, his son Ayush already asleep. Manvi always made sure the child went to bed early. He went upstairs to the bedroom. Manvi was sitting up in bed, reading a book. When Vikram entered the room, Manvi got out of bed and came over to hug him. Vikram's body tensed as if on reflex, like it did every time he returned to his wife after being with another woman.

"You've been working too hard, Vikram. You need to slow down," she kissed him lightly on his lips. Vikram felt awkward and turned away. Like always, he was afraid Manvi would smell the girl's perfume, or find out something else – something only a woman could.

"You've been drinking," Manvi looked worried as she smelt whiskey in his breath, "Have you had anything to eat?"

"Yes, I had. We dropped by a bar for a couple of drinks after work."

"Problems at work?" Manvi asked. "You don't sound too… cheerful."

"Yes. I had a long day; lots of meetings. Ashwin had to stay back as well," he regretted mentioning Ashwin the moment he uttered his name. He made a mental note to have a word with Ashwin the next morning. And that would not be the first time. Vikram had lost count of the number of times he had called upon Ashwin to cover for him, every time having to sit through a lecture on morality. "And more meetings in the morning tomorrow," Vikram added, as an excuse to end the conversation with Manvi and get to bed right away.

He kicked off his shoes, and started to unbutton his shirt.

"I'll take a shower," he said.

"Okay," Manvi picked up her book and settled under the covers, adjusting the light on the headstand.

He turned around to leave.

"Hey, weren't you going to know if you won the Evita partnership today?" Manvi asked.

Vikram usually did not discuss business at home. But he had discussed the Evita opportunity with Manvi as she was an Evita loyalist herself and Vikram had thought that it might be a good idea to run the concept by her and pick her brain.

"We didn't win. Evita decided to go with Alpha."

"Really?"

"You heard me."

"Damn! I'm sure no one saw *that* coming."

"You're right. That's the last thing we expected."

"Ashwin was on it, right?"

"Yes, he was."

"So, *that* was what all these late meetings were about?"

"Yes."

"You must be *so* pissed."

Vikram did not answer and stepped into the shower.

After the shower, he plugged the phone into a charger and put on a T-shirt and his boxer shorts.

He closed his eyes as soon as he slipped under the covers. She heard Manvi close the book, and a moment later, she turned off the light.

Manvi snuggled up to him, nuzzling her face against his neck. This was her usual overture. Tonight, it annoyed Vikram.

"Manvi…" Vikram let out a deep sigh, suggesting he was exhausted.

"Come on! You can't be *that* tired," Manvi whispered huskily in his ears, her hand on his chest under the covers. He felt her hand slide down and slip under his T-shirt.

Vikram suddenly felt angry. Manvi had, of late, developed a habit of coming on to him at the most inappropriate of times. Why the hell did she not understand? He reached down and grabbed her hand.

"Hey, something wrong?"

"Manvi, not tonight. I'm really tired."

She stopped. "Really bad day at work, huh?" Manvi tried to sound sympathetic, which further irked him.

"Yes, Manvi. I told you. Very bad," Vikram looked into her eyes as he spoke, his voice a notch higher.

Manvi got up on an elbow, and leaned over Vikram, her warm breath fanning his face. She ran a fingertip along his jaw and said, "You don't want me to cheer you up a bit?"

"I really don't, Manvi."

"Not even a little bit?"

Vikram sighed without answering.

"Are you sure, big boy?" she asked seductively, and her hand inched towards the edge of his boxers.

He reached down and grabbed her hand once again.

"Manvi, come on! Please."

Manvi chuckled. "It's only ten, darling. You can't be *that* tired!"

"I am!"

"No… you are not!"

"Manvi, damn it! I'm just not in the mood!"

"Okay, okay!" Manvi took her hand off him. She went back to her side of the bed and lay down on her back. "We hardly make love anymore, in any case!"

"That's because you're always working late into the night on the accounts of your boutique… or checking out designs in those stupid fashion magazines," Vikram knew that it was a ridiculous excuse to cover up the fact that he was no longer sexually attracted to Manvi. But it had already slipped out of his mouth.

"I'm not 'always working late'!"

"It's four or five nights every week!" Now that he had put the blame for their non-existent sex life squarely on Manvi, Vikram was not going to relent, even if he knew he was wrong.

"And that's not 'always working late'! Besides, that's my *job*, Vikram. I thought you wanted me to work!"

"I still want you to work, Manvi!"

"*This* is not what I call being supportive, Vikram!" Manvi's eyes welled up. "You're never home. You hardly spend time with Ayush. I'm the one who really has two jobs, Vikram; one at home and one outside. You do exactly as you want, just like every other goddamned man in this world."

"Manvi, I'm too tired for this right now. You are being *very* difficult."

Manvi sat up and switched on the bedside lamp.

"Oh sure, this is all *my* fault now! *I* am being difficult!"

"There you go! Now you will play the victim card. You are an oppressed woman now. A woman who's not being treated fairly."

Manvi straightened up. "Oh yes! Of course, I *am* oppressed. And exploited. And you bloody well know that!"

"Really? What the fuck makes you oppressed? Do you ever have to wash a bundle of clothes? Do you ever have to cook a meal? Do you ever have to sweep the floors? There are maids doing all that stuff for you! There's a driver taking Ayush to school and picking him up. There are tutors to teach him. There's someone being paid to do every damn thing in this house. That *does* make you an oppressed woman, indeed!" Vikram shouted.

"I can't believe this. I never thought you'd stoop so low!" Manvi looked at him, stunned. "You know what, Vikram? It's your male ego… your weak, fragile male ego that's speaking right now."

"Really? You tell me I'm the one with a fragile ego? Your ego is so fucking fragile that you cannot handle a simple rejection for sex from a tired husband, without picking a fucking fight in the middle of the fucking night about goddamned gender issues!"

Vikram paused for a few seconds and then went on, "And I'm telling you this for the last time, Manvi. Stop acting like a victim, for god's sake! You know very well where we ended up last year, thanks to your feeling 'oppressed' and 'ignored'!"

That silenced Manvi. Tears rolled down her cheeks. She sat looking at Vikram disbelievingly, her face red.

"Vikram, I'm shocked that you brought it up! I thought we had both decided that we'd put that incident behind us and move on. I'm not trying to defend myself. But you know very well that it wasn't entirely my mistake. I had my reasons. I hope you remember the situation at that time..."

"Oh yes! The 'situation' – it was all *my* fault, wasn't it? Fuck you!" Vikram got off the bed and turned to leave.

"You started this, Vikram. Now don't play the martyr by sleeping on the couch!"

He turned back. "I didn't start anything. I am in no mood to fight with you tonight, Manvi. I am exhausted, for god's sake."

"Yes, you did start it, Vikram. You were the one who started with *my* 'always working late'!"

"And you were complaining about no sex." Furious, Vikram left the room.

"Leave! Walk away! That's all that you're good at, Vikram Oberoi! You know what, Vikram? It's *not* your male ego. I was wrong. Ego has got nothing to do with gender. It comes from power. It's about authority. You have a god complex. It comes from your position at work. But, this is not your office, Vikram. This is home. This is family. I'm your wife. And it's not always about winning," Manvi paused for a moment and then said almost in whispers. "I sometimes wonder what'd happen if you were to lose everything one fine morning, your empire crumbling to pieces around you! Maybe you would turn into a better human being if your power were to abandon you. Maybe that would save my family. I so badly want to see you fall…"

Vikram slammed the door behind him and walked away.

16

"What's up, Vikram?"

Vikram shook Ashok Pandey's hand as he stepped into the cabin. Dev's business partner worked mainly from Bangalore, and made occasional visits to NexGen's office in Mumbai. He made it a point to meet Vikram every time he was in town.

Ashok slipped into the chair facing Vikram's desk. "I was with Dev. He is worried."

Vikram shifted in his chair. "Well… the last couple of quarters haven't been good."

"To say the least. And I believe you were banking heavily on a partnership with Evita, which did not work out for us." Ashok had his eyes fixed on Vikram who was beginning to feel uncomfortable.

"Yes. Evita took all of us by surprise, if you ask me."

"You know what, Vikram? You allow yourself to be taken by surprise if you are not vigilant enough," Ashok smiled wryly. "Dev and I have been discussing this for a while. We may have to make some decisions very soon about a restructuring."

"What... what kind of restructuring?" Vikram sat up straight.

Ashok bent forward.

"Well, it's too early to discuss this, Vikram. And I'll let Dev take his time to work out a plan," Ashok rubbed his hands and looked up at Vikram, "But we definitely need to be more proactive and more innovative. We need fresh ideas. And someone driven and motivated in charge of our business in India."

Vikram took a deep breath. He could feel knots inside his chest. His body was tense, and he tried hard not to show it. What was Ashok trying to suggest? Did the bosses not consider him fit for the job anymore? Vikram had no idea that NexGen's dismal performance in the last couple of quarters, especially the Evita debacle, would cost him so dearly. And for a moment, he was mad at Ashwin for messing up the opportunity they had had with Evita.

Vikram's throat was dry. He tried hard to get a grip on his mounting tension. He sipped from the glass of water on his desk and asked, "Looks like I might not have a job," Vikram smiled dryly. "So who do you have in mind, if I may ask?"

Ashok smiled and dismissed Vikram by waving his hand. "Oh come on, Vikram! It's still you who's sitting on that chair. Everyone stays, including you. We would hate to lose someone like you. You've been with us for several years and we would want you to continue for many more," Ashok went on as Vikram wondered what the old man was getting at, "But, we have to start thinking out of the box, Vikram. Basically, pull up our socks, if you know what I mean."

Vikram forced a smile and ran his fingers through his hair. Ashok leaned towards him and said, "Although, I have to tell you this. Ashwin met Dev the other day and presented a few ideas. He's a smart kid! Dev is mighty pleased with him. He thinks some of Ashwin's radical ideas may just bring us back in the game."

"Ashwin?" The question popped out of Vikram's mouth. He had no idea that Ashwin had met Dev behind his back. It did not make him happy.

"Yes. Ashwin is a smart and successful guy, Vikram. The two of you go back several years. You know him better than any of us, don't you?"

Vikram was suddenly not sure how well he knew his subordinate and ex-classmate.

Ashok stood up and shook Vikram's hands again. "Always a pleasure talking to you, Vikram. Don't worry! We'll tide over this crisis."

❖

After Ashok had left, Vikram paced up and down his room. His brow was creased as he tried to fit the pieces of the puzzle together.

There was no doubt in Vikram's mind that someone had leaked out the Evita proposal to Alpha. There were only three individuals who had access to it – Dev, Ashwin and him. The debacle had come in the wake of a couple of bad quarters, and made Vikram look his worst as the Head of India Operations. He was no longer sure if his position in the firm was secure. Ashwin, on the other hand, had already started making overtures to Dev, bypassing Vikram, who was supposed to be his boss! Ashwin's failure in the Evita deal was no longer being discussed. He had already made it up to the bosses, impressing them with his 'radical ideas'. Evita was now 'Vikram's idea gone wrong', and his bosses were already looking for someone more 'innovative' and 'more driven'. What was Vikram to make of that?

As the realization dawned on him, Vikram's heart skipped several beats. His hands and feet suddenly felt numb. He would have to keep an eye on Ashwin.

And there was only one person he could think of.

17

Vikram was in his penthouse, checking his watch restlessly, the cigarette stubs piling up inside the bowl in front of him.

The situation at work had taken an unexpected turn. He was unsettled, unable to concentrate. As he drained the glass of whiskey and made another drink for himself, he wished Sonal was around. He missed her. He had chosen to spend the evening alone in his penthouse, as he was expecting a visitor.

"I'd be damned if the bugger is on time even for once," Vikram muttered under his breath. It was already fifteen minutes past seven, the time that they had fixed for the appointment.

Vikram picked up his phone and was about to call the man he was expecting when he heard the cautious, almost surreptitious knock. There was no mistaking that one! He put the whiskey down and walked over to the door.

It, indeed, was Albert Pinto. He almost pushed Vikram aside and stepped in, as if he was being followed.

Vikram had asked Albert Pinto the first time they had met if that was his real name. And the detective had smiled meaningfully. "What's in a name, Vikram? I let my work do all the talking," he had declared. Vikram had not probed him about his name again.

Albert was a very tall man in his mid-forties. His hair was thinning at the front and came down to his shoulders at the back, long sideburns that had turned white, bushy eyebrows and bright eyes with crow's feet and a hooked nose. A somewhat shrivelled face that tapered to an almost pointed chin. He wore a brown coat and a very tight green shirt that showed a hint of a paunch, paired with blue denim pants that clung to his crotch. His heels added a few inches to his already imposing height, and the sharp pointed tip of his shoes, in his own words, "added character to his look". The room was inundated with the smell of cheap deodorant the moment he walked in.

He got about his 'business' immediately after stepping in, whistling the tune of a popular Hindi song. He closed the door of the study behind him. He walked up to Vikram's desk and unplugged the phone. He gestured at Vikram and Vikram switched his mobile phone off. He walked up to the glass window and pulled down the blinds.

Vikram watched him indifferently. He was used to this routine every time Albert visited him. "Most of what I do and say is illegal behaviour, and I do not take chances," Albert had explained his almost paranoiac obsession with privacy the first time they had met.

Having carried out his chores, Albert looked around. He looked satisfied and collapsed into the seat across Vikram. He kept up the whistling. Vikram could smell cheap alcohol.

"You look happy," Vikram commented.

Albert stopped whistling and looked up.

"I'm in love!" The corner of his lips curled in a smile.

"Really? Who's the lucky woman?"

Albert brushed off the sarcasm with a laughter that echoed in the room. "She was a client, actually."

"I thought you had a strict 'never-fuck-the-client' policy!"

"Well, you do make exceptions for seriously hot clients," Albert winked. "I'm only human, Vikram! She hired me to keep an eye on her husband… he was away from home most of the time on business tours. Turned out he was screwing his secretary… they were spending nights in hotels all over the city! I went to meet my client with pictures… that's a Friday… the husband was away, as usual. My client broke down. I tried to console her. Any gentleman in my place would. Wouldn't *you*, Vikram?"

Vikram did not speak. He was thinking if the name of Albert's client was Manvi Oberoi. The situation sounded familiar.

Albert went on, "I fixed her a couple of drinks to calm her down. One thing led to another. And we ended up spending the weekend together, barely getting out of bed. There hasn't been a single day since then when we haven't 'made love'…" Albert made quotation marks in the air with his fingers. "Never met anyone like her, you know… A bit on the heavier side… more than a handful in all the right places… and a hungry tigress in bed—"

Vikram raised a hand and gestured him to stop.

"A bit on the heavier side… more than a handful in all the right places". Certainly not Manvi. Vikram felt a load taken off his chest.

"I get it, Albert… Good for you, old boy! Shall we get down to business?" Vikram did not look particularly moved by Albert's love story.

"Sure," Albert pulled out a file from the briefcase he was carrying.

Ordinarily, hi-tech companies worked with agencies that specialized in running background checks on candidates they were about to hire. However, Vikram employed the services of Albert who had connections in all the right places, in addition to his hacking skills, that gave him access to all kinds of information about prospective hires. The other advantage of using Albert was that he worked fast, often delivering basic reports in hours. Albert's methods were illegal, no doubt. And Vikram knew, simply by hiring him for these background checks, he himself had broken a dozen laws. But, Vikram did not take chances, considering the business he was in. A product design falling in wrong hands could cost NexGen crores of rupees.

"I have good news for you," Albert said, "Your guy is clean." He started pulling out sheets from the file and handing them over to Vikram. "Raghav Dutta, twenty-four… is working with Tektronics as a programmer for more than a year. Here we go! His high school and university records… employment file from Tektronics. All good. Now, more recent stuff… credit card transactions for last two years from two different cards… mobile phone bills… bank statements… travel records… call records,"

Albert paused briefly and then went on, "I looked into the call records… a lot of calls to Kolkata, to his parents… a whole lot of calls toPune, has a girlfriend there. She works in a bank there… absolutely clean and another bunch of calls to Bangalore to an elder brother there who's in IT. No late night calls. No overseas calls. No suspicious patterns in his call records. No unexplained bank transfers. No unexplained heavy purchases. I think he's clean and you can hire him."

"Good," Vikram said, "Some of this stuff is supposed to be highly confidential."

"Right, so?"

"How did you manage to get hold of these?"

Albert smiled. "Vikram, let me remind you. You don't ask and I don't tell. That's another of my rules… and there's no exception to *this* one!"

"But, I'm surprised—"

Albert did not let Vikram finish.

"Hey, I'm the best! Isn't that why you pay me?"

"I know, but—"

"Listen. You wanted me to run a check on this guy you are hiring. You have everything you'll ever need to know. He's clean and you have proof. Anything else you need to know?"

"No!" Vikram sighed.

"In that case, I would take your leave now. I need to get some sleep! This woman is keeping me up all night these days," Albert stood up. He walked up to the window and drew the blinds up. He reconnected the desk phone. Vikram switched his mobile phone on.

"I'll send you a bill," Albert headed for the door.

"Albert, listen. I've another job for you and I need a report next week."

Albert turned around to face him. Vikram looked into his eyes and said, "Ashwin Saxena. Tail him. Round the clock. Wherever he goes, whoever he meets. And I want pictures."

18

The deep bass of the music throbbed inside Majestic, one of the most popular and spacious new auditoriums in Mumbai. Cones of light made patterns on the overcast night sky outside.

The who's who of the city was turning up in hordes. Photographers and reporters stationed outside the auditorium were racing against each other, chasing celebrities from the movie and fashion industries for photographs and sound bites. It was a big day for Evita. The Winter Collection of clothes and accessories was being launched. A-list models and Bollywood actors were going to walk the ramp.

It was also a big day for Alpha as the announcement of its collaboration with Evita for co-branded smart wearables was going to be made that evening. Evita had been promoting the event in leading dailies and on strategically placed street-side hoardings for weeks.

When Arun Sundaram was invited on stage by Evita's CEO Sunanda Jain after her welcome address, there was brief and scattered applause from the audience.

"Good evening, everyone," Arun smiled at the audience, looking dapper in his sharp suit and natty tie. "A lot of you must be wondering what brings the head of a technology company to a fashion extravaganza like this. We'll not keep you guessing too long." He gestured at Sunanda, standing next to him, to take over. Though she was on the wrong side of forty, Sunanda's svelte figure did complete justice to her clingy green evening dress with a plunging neckline. She ran her fingers through her immaculately straightened hair, and smiled back at Arun before turning to the audience.

"Ladies and gentlemen, I'm so happy and proud to announce that Evita has decided to partner with Alpha Tech to design and produce the next generation of smart wearables and accessories, like this country has never seen before," Sundana's voice was buried by roaring applause. After a brief pause, she continued, "And the first set of products we jointly produce will hit the market as part of our Winter Collection this year. So, the Evita overcoat you buy this winter will decide how warm is warm enough for you! And, if you cannot find your way around town, all it'll take is a tap on the sleeve to get directions read out to you as you drive!" Thunderous applause again. "All of these while still looking your best, the Evita way!"

"We're using pre-recorded digital videos as backdrop for the ramp for the first time ever in Mumbai. You'll get to see and feel winter in Switzerland as my models sashay down the ramp!" Sunanda spoke in Arun's ear as they left the stage and headed towards their seats.

There was a galaxy of celebrities in the front row. Some of the younger ones among them stood up and bowed before Sunanda as she made her way towards her seat. The media presence was remarkable, everyone jostling for the best view. The most popular television channels had their crew in attendance. As the show progressed, the psychedelic music was interrupted only by frenzied applause from the audience as top models and actors walked the ramp in one awe-inspiring design after another.

Evita's lead designer had just finished his bow before the ecstatic audience with all his models and walked back up the ramp, when Arun's phone buzzed. He looked at the number and smiled.

"Excuse me, got to take this one," he whispered in Sunanda's ear and stood up. He accepted the call and made his way out of the auditorium to a quieter hall outside.

"Aarti Bansal!" Arun smiled into the phone, "Always a pleasure to talk to you. I hope you don't have any more complaints about the money."

19

"May I?" Rakesh Behl pushed the door of the conference room open by a couple of inches and looked inside. Dev and Vikram were already inside, waiting for him.

Rakesh headed the Advanced Product Engineering group and was the chief architect of NexGen's immensely successful products. He had been working for NexGen since the early days of the company. On a number of occasions, competitors had tried to copy his designs and had ended up paying heavy damages for intellectual property violations in lawsuits all over the world.

Rakesh looked at the panoramic view of Mumbai through the glass wall of the conference room. The evening traffic on the road below was sluggish. The street lights along Marine Drive looked like tiny yellow dots on the black canvas of the sky from the twenty-first floor.

"Rakesh, come right in!" Dev smiled warmly, "We were worried you had left already! I have something very important to discuss with you."

Rakesh pulled a chair and sat next to Vikram, across the table from Dev.

"Rakesh, Vikram and I have been toying with the idea of a merger with Quantum Technologies in Japan for a while now."

"With Quantum in Japan?" Rakesh asked, looking somewhat bewildered.

"Let me explain," Dev kept his eyes on Rakesh, and reclined on his chair. "We all agree that we need to expand to global markets, right? But, establishing a brand in a new country is a long-drawn-out process. Going to a market along with an established local company is a much quicker option," Dev explained. "Also, as we all can see, the world today is shrinking. We need to pick up best practices from other regions if we want to be a global player. Now, instead of trying to put together entirely new manufacturing, marketing and sales teams in a new country, it is a better idea to work with a local partner and leverage *their* capabilities. On the other hand, in the domestic market, there is an increasing demand for foreign products not currently available in India. It will make sense for us to sell Quantum's products in the Indian market and cater to that demand as well."

"That's a great idea, Dev! But why would Quantum be interested? It seems to me that *we* are the ones who are set to benefit more from the merger," Rakesh sounded sceptical.

"Good question, Rakesh. Let me tell you how Quantum benefits from this. Quantum is a medium sized company. They have a highly competent technical workforce and knowledge of the local market, but their cash reserves are limited. And, they are being beaten black and blue on their home turf by a global giant like Alpha. That's where we come in. We bring in our technical expertise, we pump in cash to scale up their research, manufacturing and marketing, and we help drive sales better than what Quantum is capable of doing on its own right now. Also, as I said just now, we are also helping them enter the Indian market."

"I see," Rakesh nodded. "So, what's the plan?" he asked.

"Vikram, why don't you take over from here?" Dev gestured to Vikram. "This is your baby!"

Vikram turned to Rakesh.

"Rakesh, in my view, the success of this will depend on how effectively we exchange technical know-how and standardize processes between the two companies. Also, we need to have a first-hand view of their operations. Do they conform to our standards? If not, how much investment do *we* need to make to help them scale up?"

He continued after a brief pause, "We just got off a call with their CEO and their product engineering head. They are ready to get into a workshop with us to discuss new product designs where there are opportunities for collaboration. Also, if we have someone on ground zero at Tokyo, we will get the chance to check out their manufacturing plants in Japan, and Dev is already drawing up an aggressive marketing plan for that region. The question now is, how soon can *you* fly to Tokyo, Rakesh, with the new designs that you're currently working on?"

"So, if I understand correctly, you want me to fly down to Tokyo with the new designs I am working on, and get into a workshop with Quantum."

"That's right, Rakesh!" Vikram confirmed.

"Won't that be risky?"Rakesh asked, "Exposing our designs so early…"

"Well, as for Quantum, we are drafting the appropriate terms of confidentiality. We will need to make sure the designs don't end up in the wrong hands. I have also instructed the engineering teams from Quantum to be vigilant. They have walked us through their security and confidentiality provisions and they look pretty solid."

Rakesh nodded in agreement.

"So how soon can you fly, Rakesh?" Vikram asked again.

"Rakesh, consider this our last shot at making a comeback," Dev sounded tired, trying to drive home the criticality of the assignment. Vikram himself was acutely conscious of what the failure of their plans in Japan would mean for his own future. That was probably the last chance Dev had offered him to salvage his position in the firm.

Rakesh's messy divorce proceedings had just ended. Getting away from Mumbai for a while sounded like a good idea. He looked up and smiled at Vikram, "I'm ready, Vikram! I can catch a flight as soon as the travel arrangements are complete."

"I'll speak to Sonal tomorrow. She'll take care of your travel arrangements. Thanks Rakesh, and, all the best!"

Dev and Vikram stood up and took turns in shaking hands with Rakesh.

Rakesh walked out of the conference room, and almost ran into Aarti who was standing right outside the door.

"Hey Rakesh… Vikram is inside, isn't he?" She held up a file she was carrying, "He wanted this before he left for the day," she offered an unsolicited explanation.

"Yes, he's inside… I was with him." Rakesh smiled and walked away, wondering why Aarti had looked startled for a fleeting second.

20

Vikram kept staring at the ceiling and smoked quietly. Sonal lay next to him, covered up to her neck by the white sheet, her eyes fixed on him. They had made love twice since afternoon, and Vikram now looked tired and somewhat distant, lost in his thoughts.

"Is everything alright?" Sonal finally asked, placing her hand on his.

Despite their physical intimacy, Vikram had carefully avoided opening his heart to Sonal. He was, by nature, a private person, usually choosing to keep his emotions bottled up inside. The insecurities, the fears, the demons inside were for him and only him to battle. He neither encouraged nor liked intrusion into his fiercely protected emotional space.

However, there was something in the way Sonal had put that question that he felt something snap inside. His heart suddenly felt heavy and he wanted to share a bit of that load with the woman lying next to him, ready to lend an ear to his worries.

"Well… things could've been better at work, sweetheart," he finally said.

Sonal sat up, surprised by Vikram's uncharacteristic candour. She passed an arm around his shoulder and snuggled closer to him. She said, "I guessed. I see you restless in the office these days. You probably haven't noticed but you lose your temper quite easily these days, Vikram. And to be honest, you're grumpy most of the time... not quite the charmer that you earlier were."

"You're right, I guess," Vikram sighed and took a sip of the red wine from the glass on the bedside table. "The firm hasn't been doing too well. Dev is not happy. And I don't know whom to trust!"

"Ashwin was telling me that the Evita deal has fallen through…"

"Oh yes, it has. And he is sure someone among us leaked out the proposal to Alpha!"

"What do *you* think?"

"I… I don't know, Sonal!" Vikram sounded helpless.

"I should probably not be saying this, but I heard rumours in the office that Ashwin had been eyeing the country head position when *you* got promoted and he lost the race…"

"That's what I've heard too," Vikram smiled wryly.

"Do you think he might have sabotaged the deal to make *you* look bad?"

Vikram's jaws stiffened. It was funny that Sonal was also considering that possibility. Was it *that* obvious, even to someone like her, who was not connected with the deal in any way?

He said after a pause, "I'll figure that out soon enough, if he is indeed trying to act smart," and then looked at Sonal with a smile. "You know what? It's actually quite nice talking to you."

"I'm happy you think that way." Sonal smiled back warmly. "You can always talk to me, Vikram."

"I really don't open up with anyone, you know. Manvi and I hardly connect, if you know what I mean," Vikram went on. Sonal was taken aback by the information Vikram had just volunteered. They had never discussed his wife before this. She wondered if it was the wine talking.

"There's always this… this emptiness that I'm looking to fill," Vikram went on, his voice almost reduced to whispers. Sonal had her head on his shoulder, running her fingers through the hair on his chest. A part of Vikram hated himself for letting his demons out before Sonal. Another part of him felt lighter and happier. "And there's a sense of contentment when I'm with you," he ran his fingers carelessly through Sonal's hair and kissed her forehead.

"Do I take that as a compliment?" Sonal looked up from his chest into his eyes and beamed.

"I guess you can." Vikram laughed.

"Till you move on to the next hottie who crosses your path," Sonal looked away from him, freeing herself from his arms.

Vikram pulled her back on his chest. He did not know why, but suddenly, chasing 'the next hottie who crossed his path' did not seem like a great idea anymore.

For days, Vikram had been dreaming of a life with Sonal, away from all the madness, of a small house he could call home, of lazy evenings filled with music and laughter and stories of their childhood, of messing around in the kitchen trying to cook their favourite dishes, and of endless nights of passionate lovemaking. Why, he might actually enjoy accompanying Sonal on a shopping binge buying for her everything that wealth could buy, or even carrying bags of grocery for her! So not like the Vikram Oberoi he knew.

And for the hundredth time that day, Vikram felt that his search had ended with Sonal.

❖

Manvi looked up from her laptop and her eyes went to the clock. She had been engrossed in her work and it was already eight. It was time to get Ayush ready for dinner.

That was when her phone rang. She did not recognize the number.

"Am I speaking to Ms Manvi Oberoi?"

Manvi could not recognize the voice either. It was a woman on the other end of the line.

"Yes, I'm Manvi. And who am I speaking to?"

"That's not really important, Ms Oberoi. What's important is for you to know where Mr Vikram Oberoi is right now."

21

Rakesh walked into the aircraft headed for Tokyo with mixed feelings. On the one hand, this being his first trip to Japan, Rakesh was looking forward to an opportunity to soak in a unique culture, enjoy the Japanese cuisine and probably get a taste of the kinky Tokyo night-life that he had only read and heard about. Thanks to the divorce proceedings over the last several months, Rakesh had purposely stayed away from female company and had lived like a celibate.

On the other hand, he knew the stakes of his business travel. With the Evita partnership gone sour, the future of NexGen depended largely on the success of his Tokyo trip. He had with him the new designs that he had been working on.

As Rakesh settled down in an aisle seat mulling over the implications of his trip, he was distracted by a sensuous perfume up close. He looked up and saw the girl. She was in a hot-pink top, and clingy jeans that accentuated her full hips. One look at her and Rakesh's jaw dropped. It seemed the air had been sucked out of his innards.

"Hi, could you please help me with this bag?"

The girl was struggling to put what looked like a pretty heavy bag up in the overhead locker right above his seat. Rakesh was only too happy to oblige.

It turned out that she had the seat next to him. "Thank you so much," said the girl as she slid past Rakesh and took up the seat by the window.

"I'm Amyra," the girl extended a hand after she had taken her seat.

"Rakesh," it took Rakesh a while to let go of her hand.

Over the next few hours, they got to know each other. Amyra worked for a travel magazine and was visiting Tokyo on an assignment. She, in turn, was thrilled to make her acquaintance with a 'Tech Guru' – as she chose to call Rakesh – who designed smartphones! "How cool is that!" Amyra exclaimed in almost childlike fervour when she found out what Rakesh did for a living.

During the flight, Rakesh could feel mounting sexual tension and wondered if it was only him, as his heart skipped a beat every time their bodies made contact in the closed space.

When the cabin lights were dimmed after dinner, Amyra pushed her seat back and curled up under her blanket. Rakesh tried to get some sleep, but he was too restless for a mid-air nap with his hormones raging.

22

Sonal checked her watch one more time and wondered whether she should call Prachi. She was in the coffee shop right outside the NexGen tower. Prachi had wanted to meet her after work. "Preferably outside the office," she had added. Sonal had suggested the coffee shop. Sonal now wondered if Prachi would be able to make it. She was already late by almost half an hour.

That was when Prachi pushed open the glass door of the coffee shop and walked in. She dumped her bag on an empty chair next to their table.

"Phew! I'm so sorry, Sonal. How long have you been waiting?" Prachi looked genuinely apologetic.

"About twenty minutes." Sonal smiled. She was still trying to figure out what this clandestine meeting outside the office was about.

"That time of the year, darling! Everyone's going crazy with the yearly appraisals, and all the mathematics around bonuses and pay hikes!" Prachi rolled her eyes. "Have no idea how much *I* am going to make this year, though!"

They both laughed.

"Hey, have you ordered?" Prachi asked.

"No… was waiting for you," Sonal smiled.

Prachi gestured at the waiter.

"I'll have a frappe… with extra chocolate sauce… and a brownie with ice cream," Prachi shifted in her chair. She never bothered about the steadily accumulating kilos. "I'm very hungry," she winked at Sonal.

"A cappuccino for me… and two oatmeal cookies," Sonal decided.

When the waiter departed, Prachi turned to face Sonal.

"So Sonal, how's it going?"

"The usual… work keeps me busy. And I'm not complaining."

There was a moment's silence between them. And then, Prachi spoke.

"Sonal, you must be wondering why I wanted to talk to you," Prachi's eyes were fixed on Sonal. She saw Sonal shift uncomfortably in her seat and said, "Sonal, the only reason why I wanted to meet outside the office is that I want you to relax. Look at this as two girls catching up after work." Prachi smiled warmly. Sonal smiled tentatively.

"Sonal, let me come straight to the point," Prachi was looking into Sonal's eyes, "What's going on between Vikram and you?"

Sonal looked away. The sun had set, and the lights inside Hi-Tech Park had come up. She could see men and women with their backpacks queueing up for the office buses that would drop them home; men and women whose lives were probably much simpler than hers.

The waiter came back with their order and laid out the food and beverages on the table.

After the waiter had left, Sonal looked at Prachi. "What have *you* heard, Prachi?"

"Sonal, I don't usually lend my ears to gossip. I want to hear it from *you*," Prachi sounded compassionate.

"Well, we…" Sonal took a few seconds to find the right words, "We are seeing each other."

"You are?" Prachi bent forward, picking up her glass of frappe. "So, there's truth in what everyone's saying."

"I guess, yes." Sonal shrugged matter-of-factly, sipping her coffee.

"Sonal, how well do you know Vikram Oberoi?" Prachi almost spat out the words, looking into Sonal's eyes.

Sonal opened her mouth to say something, and then held back. Instead she said, "Prachi, I'm not sure where we're going with this."

"Sonal, I'm only trying to make you see some sense here. You know, Vikram is married, don't you?"

"Yes, I know."

"And it doesn't bother you that he'll *never* walk out of his marriage and he's having a fling with you on the side? A very public fling at that, which may ruin your career!"

"Prachi, look… I really appreciate your concern. But, what Vikram and I share is very important to us. It's very precious. I'd be very happy if you don't insult our relationship by calling it a fling," Sonal retorted.

"You know, Vikram was dating Aarti just the other day?"

"Yes, I've heard that."

"And have you seen her these days, Sonal? She's a broken woman! She went too deep into that relationship. She used to think and behave just the way *you* are doing right now, Sonal. And you can see what Vikram has done to her. Don't you realize, Sonal? Vikram is not the kind of man you can trust!"

"Prachi, are you suggesting that my relationship with Vikram will not work out, just because it didn't work out with Aarti?"

"Relationship?" Prachi smiled, "Oh Sonal! You are too young... and too naïve," Prachi put her hand on Sonal's. "You don't know sharks like Vikram Oberoi. I do. I've been around too long, and I've seen too many of them. And I am worried about you. I don't want you to end up like Aarti."

Sonal withdrew her hand and finished her coffee.

"Prachi, I can't thank you enough for worrying about me. For making the time from your busy schedule to see me and to talk to me. To warn me. But Vikram and I are serious about this. I don't care if he is married. I don't care if he has dated a dozen women in the past and none of them was good enough for him. All I know is that I love him and he loves me; we will make this work. And we give a damn to what the world says about us!"

As Sonal stormed out of the coffee shop, Prachi looked around and lowered her head, shaking it in disbelief.

23

Rakesh was spoilt for choice as he browsed through the list of restaurants and bars in his hotel in Kinshicho. Kinshicho was one of the busy industrial areas in Tokyo. It had also made a name for itself over the years for its several shopping arcades and throbbing night-life.

Amyra had checked in to the same hotel and had gone out by herself in the evening. Rakesh had spent a good part of the evening in his room figuring out the rather unique functioning of the fully-automated Japanese toilet seat, quite a revelation in its own right for a foreigner. And then he had been in the 7-Eleven store in the basement of the hotel, stocking up on supplies and withdrawing cash. Finally, he spent some time working on his presentation to the Quantum team the next morning, before he left his room to get dinner.

As he walked in to a Japanese restaurant in the hotel, he was pleasantly surprised to discover that the restaurant was sparsely crowded. The diners were mostly those who were staying in the same hotel.

No sooner had Rakesh ordered a Japanese whiskey than Amyra appeared before his table. She was in a short summer dress, navy blue with white polka dots. Her hair was tied back. Amyra had been out roaming the busy Kinshicho streets and the shopping malls for quite some time. The evening was warm. Her cheeks were flushed.

"May I?"Amyra smiled at Rakesh as she pulled a chair.

Later that night, inside Rakesh's room, when Amyra came out of the washroom, she stood still for a few seconds, as she watched Rakesh in bed, holding the covers up, gesturing an invitation for her to join him.

As Amyra slid under the covers, Rakesh took her in his arms, feeling her soft warmth all over. He could taste the mint in her mouth as he kissed her. Her hand slipped under his tee and caressed his back.

Rakesh's laptop with the product designs was on the study desk, still turned on.

24

As the first rays of the sun seeped in through the cracks in the curtains, Rakesh opened his eyes. His arm was around Amyra. She was still asleep, her smooth bare back on his chest, his nose nuzzled in her hair. He made her turn around and kissed her deep and long, running his fingers through her hair.

"Hungry already?"she whispered sleepily.

"Good morning," Rakesh whispered as he pulled her closer, feeling the warm fullness of her breasts on his chest.

She felt his hands on her body – fondling her, caressing her all over. She freed herself and ran to the washroom, without bothering to pick up her dress that still lay on the carpet where it had been carelessly tossed the night before. A couple of minutes later, she opened the washroom door just a bit. She peeped through the narrow opening and beckoned Rakesh inside with a finger.

Rakesh knew he was getting late. "What the hell! Maybe I'll skip breakfast," he muttered to himself as he sprang out of bed, uncontrollably aroused, and rushed to join Amyra in the washroom.

❖

Amyra was the first to leave the washroom in her bathing gown, leaving Rakesh to finish his bath. In the room, she rushed to the table where Rakesh's laptop was propped up. The battery had died. She quickly connected the battery charger and booted the laptop.

She logged in as an Administrator. She pulled out her phone. She was looking for the Administrator password that she had saved in a note in her phone.

It had taken some more cash and another clandestine rendezvous in a hotel room with Agastya, who now seriously considered Ruchika a 'hot girlfriend' and had also started taking pride in his role in a 'covert mission' to expose a 'big financial scam that would blow up any day now'. The password to the Administrator account for every laptop in the firm was in the safe custody of the Network and Systems team.

Once logged in, Amyra searched the disk for files or folders with the word 'Tokyo' in the name and it took her a few seconds to find a folder named <TOKYO WORKSHOP>. She fished out a pen drive from her purse and made a copy of the contents of the folder, looking behind her shoulder every now and then to see if Rakesh had stepped out of the bath.

When the contents of the folder had been copied, she shut the laptop down and disconnected the charger, leaving the laptop just the way she had found it.

25

Amyra was to meet them in half an hour in a suite in the Marriott at Kinshicho.

As the taxi made its way towards the hotel through rush-hour traffic, Amyra thought about the possible reasons her patron might have had. She wondered how someone could be so intent on destroying someone else. After all these years in the profession and meeting all kinds of people, human nature never ceased to surprise her!

In addition to the unbelievable amount of money she was being paid, her trip to Tokyo had also been paid for. The sex with Rakesh the previous night, by the way, had been beyond anything she had ever experienced. She wished she could stay in touch with that man. He did mention last night that he was single now, after his divorce with his wife.

But that was not to be. Her job was not just to seduce

Rakesh, but also to hand over the files she had copied from his laptop sometime back, to the men who would be waiting for her in that suite in the Marriott. After handing over the designs, she would have to back off from all of this for good, like all this had never happened at all.

❖

The door leading to the suite was opened for her after the second knock. Amyra was ushered into a room where three Japanese men were seated.

The senior-most was a short, stout and unassuming looking man with a crew-cut. He greeted her with a bow. She reciprocated. She did not know his name, and she really did not care.

"It is good to see you, though you are five minutes late," the man spoke in broken English. "We were wondering if you would leave your lover's room at all." He laughed. The two other younger men in the room joined him. The men were already getting on Amyra's nerves.

"I made a promise. And I intend to keep it." Amyra handed the leader the pen drive. He, in turn, tossed the pen drive in the direction of one of his men, signalling at him to go through its contents. The man plugged it in to a laptop that was propped up on a desk in the room.

For the next few minutes, the man bent over the desk, his brow creased, his eyes reduced to tiny slits. Amyra looked impatiently at her watch a couple of times. She could feel the hungry eyes of the other two men all over her body. When their eyes met, the older man smiled at her and gestured at her, offering her a seat. She was in no mood to make herself comfortable inside that suite and could not wait to leave.

After some time, the man at the desk flashed his thumb at the older man. He looked back at her and said, "Looks like you have done your job well! Thank you very much." He bowed.

❖

As soon as she walked out of the hotel, Amyra dialled a number in Mumbai.

"The job is done. I've handed everything over to the Jap guys."

Then she added with a wicked grin on her face, "Are you sure I cannot see this guy again? Maybe just one last time before I fly out?"

26

Vikram looked at his watch. It was 6:55 in the evening. Albert Pinto was supposed to be there at seven. He looked around at the teeming crowd on the Chowpatty beach and at the gaudily decked-up stalls by the beach selling *chaats* and *pao-bhaji*. He saw people renting straw mats by the hour and sitting by the water, lovers getting cozy in the balmy evening air. It was always easy to steal a few private moments in a crowd. Vikram's eyes went to the arc of the Marine Drive, and at the specks of variously coloured lights in the horizon. The wind swept through his hair, as cars swooshed down the road in front of him. Vikram was anxious to find out what Albert had to report.

Albert waved at Vikram from across the road and then crossed over, once the traffic had stopped with the lights turning red.

"Good evening, Vikram!" he sounded tired. The spring in his step which Vikram had noticed the last time was also gone.

"Good evening, Albert. Everything okay?"

"Why do you ask?"

"You don't look very cheerful. Anything wrong?"

"I'm nursing a broken heart," Albert pointed at his chest with his thumb. He brushed back with his fingers a few strands of grey hair that had landed on his forehead in the breeze. He had a day-old stubble that was more salt than pepper.

"Why? What happened?"

"You remember the woman I told you about?"

"You mean the tigress who was keeping you up all night?"

"Yeah… that's the one."

"What happened to her?"

"She went to her husband and told him that she had come to know about his affair… wanted a divorce… the husband apologized… no one wants to pay settlement money, you know… he said it had been a mistake that he would never repeat… she bought that… she came to me and told me that *our* affair had also been a mistake that *she* would never repeat… and now the two are off to Europe on a long vacation."

"That's sad, Albert. Did she pay you?"

"Actually, she still owes me a few thousands…" Albert's face darkened.

"Never mind. You had a good time with her, didn't you?"

Albert ran his fingers through his hair. His eyes had a distant look. "It wasn't just a fling, Vikram. I thought I had fallen in love. Finally…"

"Albert, I understand your pain," Vikram paused briefly and then said, "Let's talk business. Have you been able to get anything on Ashwin?"

Albert sighed and then spoke in a business-like tone, "Yes, let's talk business."

He pulled out his phone, went to the photo gallery, and started swiping through pictures and talking about them.

"Mostly business meetings during the day... a couple of business dinners... I have made a list of clients and business associates he has been meeting... you probably know most of these people already... weekends mostly with the family... beautiful wife and an absolutely adorable daughter... in shopping malls, movies, restaurants... nothing you should really be worried about. No reason to think he's looking for a change, if that's what's bothering you. I'd say he's not talking to anyone you don't want him to."

Albert was almost at the end of the collection of pictures, when he stopped.

"And these... you probably know about these lunch meetings already... considering he's also a family-friend..."

Vikram's heart sank when he looked at the last six pictures. He took the phone from Albert's hand and swiped through them once again.

Ashwin had been with Manvi. Vikram checked the dates of the photos. Twice during the last seven days. And Vikram had no clue.

"Maybe you would turn into a better human being if your power were to abandon you. Maybe that would save my family. I so badly want to see you fall..." Manvi's words echoed in Vikram's mind.

"Ashwin, what are you up to now?" Vikram whispered under his breath, "And what business does my wife have with you?"

27

In another part of the city, Aarti Bansal sat alone at a bar. As she looked around after ordering another large whiskey on the rocks, she realized that she had had a few too many. There seemed to be a pall of mist around the gyrating figures on the dance floor, the music seemed to be floating in from somewhere far away. The faces of men who came up to her at regular intervals and tried to make small talk looked blurred in the whiskey fog that was fast taking over her senses. She could only see their lips moving.

Aarti looked at people drinking and dancing in frenzy on the floor. She looked at the women – happy women, basking in the affection of the men surrounding them. She wished she could talk sense into their muddled-up minds. She wanted to scream and tell them that, they would all end up alone – eventually.

The whiskey always made her philosophical. Her senses were fast giving up. She was finding it difficult to keep her eyes open.

Aarti picked up her glass and tottered out through a side door into the open-air lounge next to the disco. It was warm and humid. She slumped into a chair and threw her head back, looking at the stars that suddenly seemed closer than ever.

She whispered, "Vikram, I know you are falling hard… very hard! It was tough luck with Evita, wasn't it? And there'll be more, you bastard! You know what? You shouldn't have left Aarti Bansal for that bitch! I will finish you!"

28

It was around nine in the night when Vikram walked into a quiet house, as always.

He clutched his phone. Albert had sent him the pictures by WhatsApp a while back. As he trudged up the staircase, Vikram smiled at the unexpected turn of fate. He had always been apprehensive about Manvi finding out about his dalliances outside their marriage. He had never imagined himself having to confront Manvi with evidence of her secret lunch meetings with an ex-lover, who Vikram was now sure had hatched a conspiracy against him in the office.

As he walked into the bedroom, he saw Manvi busy removing her clothes from the cupboard and putting them on the bed in neat piles.

"What's going on?" Vikram asked.

"Nothing that would bother you," Manvi replied curtly, without bothering to look at Vikram.

"Looks like you have your own ideas about what bothers me and what doesn't!"

"Learning from you, Vikram," Manvi turned to face him. "Good that you're home on time, for a change. I've something to tell you. I've decided to—"

"Manvi, keep that attitude aside for a while, will you?" Vikram did not let Manvi finish. He unlocked his phone with his pattern and went straight to WhatsApp. He pulled up the pictures Albert had sent him a while back.

He took a few steps towards Manvi and raised the phone, so that it was now level with Manvi's eyes.

"Care to tell me what *these* are about?"

Manvi looked unperturbed. She did not answer his question. Instead, her eyes went to the name of the sender of the pictures and she looked at Vikram in the eyes.

"'Albert'?" Manvi read out the name aloud, "Who's Albert?"

"How does that matter?" Vikram grimaced, "I've asked you a question and you better come clean!"

"Come clean?" Manvi laughed out. "Look who's talking!"

"Manvi, I *demand* you to tell me what Ashwin and you have been up to behind my back."

"Why do you ask, Vikram? Are you jealous? I thought you wouldn't care even if you saw me fucking someone right under your nose!"

"Manvi, you need to know that Ashwin—"

"What about him? Now he's the bad guy, is he?" Manvi did not let Vikram finish.

"Let's just say that he's trying to act smart," Vikram muttered under his breath. "I cannot and need not tell you more than that. And now, when I see these pictures, I wonder if the two of you together—"

"Vikram, tell me the truth," Manvi smirked, "for a change!"

"What do you want to know?"

"You are afraid that Ashwin has let your secrets out, aren't you?"

"What… what do you mean?" Vikram swallowed hard. What secrets was Manvi talking about?

"I'll come to that later, Vikram. Who's Albert?"

Vikram did not answer.

"Okay, let me guess. A fucking detective? You hired someone to keep an eye on me, you fucking asshole?"

"It's not how you think it is, Manvi—"

"How dare you get someone to tail me, you dirty pig?"

"He wasn't tailing you. He was after Ashwin. And it's an office thing…" Vikram's hand now held on to the chair for support. The conversation was not going the way he had planned. Why did he have to offer an explanation? "You haven't answered my question yet, Manvi," Vikram tried to sound firm.

"What do you want to know, Vikram? I'm not even sure where I should start from!" Manvi thought for a while and said, "This started a few days back. It was around eight in the evening. I was getting ready to feed Ayush when I received a call. From a woman I did not know. She said that you were with another girl at that very moment—"

"A woman? She called you up and spoke bullshit about me. And you didn't bother to find out who she was, or even check with me?"

"Well, if you *have* to know, she abruptly ended the call before I could ask her who she was. And as for checking with you, are you sure you would've told me the truth had I asked you?" Manvi picked up a bottle of water and took a generous slug. Her face was flushed, and she was shivering with rage.

"Of course!"

"Are you sure, Vikram? You'd tell me the truth *every time* she called me?"

"What do you mean? She called you again?"

"She called me every evening after that first call, Vikram!"

"What the hell! And you never bothered to check?"

"I did, you horny bastard! I did!" Manvi screamed, "But I didn't check with you, as I knew that'd get me nowhere. I called Ashwin instead."

"Ah, your ex-flame? Not 'ex' anymore, is he?"

"Shut up, you filthy dog! Not every man is a lecher like you. When I met Ashwin and wanted to find out what you've been up to behind my back, he decided to value his friendship way more than his loyalty towards his scheming, cunning boss!"

"Manvi, I'm surprised! Here I am, holding evidence of you hanging out with an ex-lover behind my back – an ex-lover who, by the way, is also trying to screw me at the office – and you're the one who's shouting and calling me a lecher?"

"Ashwin has told me everything!"

"What do you mean?" Vikram's voice wavered.

"About your ways, Vikram. I've been trying so hard to forget what happened last year. I took your word for it. I thought you had changed. But, I was so wrong. You're a fucking liar! You can look into someone's eyes and lie through your teeth without feeling anything." Manvi was now screaming.

"Manvi, you don't have to trust everything Ashwin says!"

Manvi did not answer. She grabbed Vikram's collars and went on, her voice almost reduced to a hiss, "What should I not believe, Vikram? That you tell him to cover up for you every time you come home late after fucking someone, with excuses of late meetings? That you've been using him as an alibi? That you carried on with Aarti for months after you had told me that it was a mistake and that it was all over between the two of you? That there are these random hookers you pick up from bars around the city and take them to your penthouse? And now, there's a new girl in the office who's warming your bed. Sonal!"

"Ashwin, you bastard!" Vikram looked away and muttered under his breath, his free hand balled into a fist.

"Stop cursing him, Vikram! Doesn't suit you... doesn't suit you at all!" Manvi's slap landed hard on Vikram's cheek. And then, another on the other cheek. She went on slapping him in frenzy.

"Manvi, this is all bullshit! Ashwin is trying to make me look bad. At work. At home. He's trying to fuck with my mind..." Vikram's feeble defence rung hollow in his ears.

Manvi raised a hand and gestured him to stop. Without another word, she went back to the pile of clothes. Vikram noticed there was a trolley bag that stood next to the bed. Manvi pulled it up, unzipped it and started dumping her clothes inside.

"Manvi, what do you think you're doing?"

Manvi looked at Vikram in the eyes.

"Don't you realize, you idiot! I'm leaving you. And don't you dare try to stop me. I'm not going to change my mind!" Manvi zipped up the bag and stood up straight. "Oh, and those pics in your phone... you can shove them up that detective's ass. You didn't manage to scare me with those. I was going to tell you, in any case, about my lunch meetings with Ashwin and every single thing that I've come to know during those meetings."

There was a call on Manvi's phone. She walked past Vikram to get it. Vikram turned around and saw Ayush at the bedroom door, all dressed up. His eyes were wide as he had been trying to make sense of what had been going on between his parents inside their bedroom. When their eyes met, he smiled sweetly at Vikram.

Vikram heard Manvi's side of the conversation on the phone.

"Yes Dad, I'm ready."

"No. You don't have to come inside."

"Wait inside the car. I'll come down with Ayush in a minute..."

29

"I'm not going to go down on my knees and plead with Manvi to come back," Vikram lighted a cigarette and took a long drag. He passed an arm around Sonal and pulled her to his chest. They reclined on a divan in the balcony of his penthouse. It was late in the night. There was a light drizzle, and the moist breeze caressed their faces.

"Are you sure, Vikram?" Sonal looked into Vikram's eyes.

"I'm absolutely sure, Sonal. I was going to tell her about us, in any case. It's sad that she had to hear from someone else."

"What happens next, Vikram?" Sonal asked, her head resting on Vikram's chest, her eyes wandering uncertainly to the trees tossing their heads in the wind.

Vikram kissed her on her head. "Don't you realize, stupid girl? Our time has finally come!"

"Are you sure about this?" Sonal looked up and asked once again, with an impish grin. "You are a free man now. And there's not going to be any dearth of women who would throw themselves at you!"

"I've only two words for them – I'm taken!"

"Oh, you are? And who's that lucky bitch?" Sonal said mockingly.

"A certain Miss Verma!" Vikram laughed.

Sonal sat up straight and said, "Listen, if that's your idea of proposing to me, I'm not going to fall for it, okay? I need a proper proposal!"

"In due time, sweetheart!" Vikram bent towards her and they kissed, as the skies rumbled.

"But how did Manvi find out about us?" Sonal asked after they had broken the kiss.

"Ashwin told her. They have been meeting behind my back. They used to be college sweethearts, you know," Vikram took another drag of his cigarette and added, "I won't be surprised if Ashwin is fucking her."

"How do you know that Ashwin and Manvi have been meeting?" Sonal's voice betrayed her surprise.

"I have my sources." Vikram smiled with a wink.

"And why do you think Ashwin would tell her about us?"

"Don't you get it, Sonal? Ashwin is on a fucking mission to destroy me! Sabotaging my business plans, sucking up to my bosses, bitching about me to my wife – the bastard is trying every trick in the book to mess me up completely! He knows very well that if my personal life is fucked up, my work will suffer as well. He's jealous, and he's eyeing my chair. He wants to see me fall!" Vikram stood up. He was suddenly very angry, "God! I need a drink!"

As Vikram headed for the bar, Sonal ran after him. She hugged him from behind. "Calm down, Vikram. Just calm down, okay? You have me and you know that. I'll always be by your side. We'll fight this out, together."

Vikram turned around and looked into Sonal's eyes. He loved her, and he believed her. He knew that she would be by his side. But this was not her battle. It was his battle and he would have to bleed alone.

"I'm so tired, Sonal," Vikram said.

Sonal ran her fingers through his hair and said, "I know, baby. Come, let's go to bed."

30

It had been two weeks since Manvi left, and Vikram had not been able to confront Ashwin with the damning pictures and demand an explanation. And that was not just because Ashwin had been away on a business trip and Vikram wanted to have the conversation face-to-face, preferably outside the office, but also because Ashwin was an important, almost indispensable member of his team and Vikram was afraid that the personal animosity between them might have negative repercussions on the already dwindling fortunes of NexGen.

At the same time, if Ashwin was playing games behind his back, Vikram had to confront him and find out everything about what Ashwin was up to. Especially about the woman who had been calling up Manvi regularly.

Who the hell was that? Ashwin probably knew, if he had been trying to set him up.

The opportunity presented itself in a way Vikram had not foreseen.

❖

Vikram was sitting at the bar in Poison. The place was noisy, filled with the evening business crowd. He felt a hand on his shoulder and looked up. Dev was standing by the bar, smiling at him. He saw Ashwin standing a few paces behind.

Vikram stood up.

Dev shook hands with Vikram.

"Vikram, good to see you here. How are you coping with all this?"

"*All this?*" Vikram squinted his eyes.

Dev smiled wryly and said, "I heard about Manvi and Ayush. Not to mention, the difficult times we're all going through at work."

"I'm okay," Vikram said, wondering who had told Dev about Manvi and Ayush leaving him. Was it Ashwin?

"Good for you," Dev placed his hand on Vikram's shoulder, almost in a paternal manner. He then said, "Vikram, listen! There's a quiet booth in the corner over there. I've ordered a few drinks there. We can talk for a while. Is that okay?"

"That'd be fine," Vikram jerked his shoulders. He was very familiar with the angry, loud-mouthed Dev. This extremely polite and cautious version made him slightly uncomfortable and apprehensive.

Vikram glanced at Ashwin. Ashwin smiled at him and raised a hand in greeting. Vikram nodded, not smiling.

They followed Dev to the booth.

Once inside, Dev settled into the leather-padded chair and faced Vikram.

"Well, Vikram. We go back a long way, you and I."

"Yes, Dev. We do, indeed," Vikram wondered where this was going.

"And Ashwin and you have known each other for even longer. The two of you went to the same college, right?"

"We've been partners in a lot of unmentionable crimes," Ashwin winked and laughed out loud, joined by Dev.

"I'd rather not ask you about *those*," Dev winked back at Ashwin.

If the two were trying to lighten the air, their jest was having no effect on Vikram.

Dev's eyes went back to Vikram. "So, Vikram," he watched Vikram carefully, "the point is, we're all friends here. So, let's keep formalities out of the door, and let's talk like friends. I'm not going to bullshit you by beating about the bush. And I promise, none of us is going to be judgemental. So, we can all be honest with one another."

Dev paused for a few seconds and then continued, "Vikram, we have problems in the company, and as I've been telling you, we've got to take care of them, before they turn into a big mess for all of us. Do not take this personally, but I can only appeal to your superior judgement to figure out what we're going to do about these problems."

"Dev, you said you were not going to beat about the bush…" Vikram sounded impatient.

"And I won't. Look, Vikram. It's no secret that you enjoy the good life. And what you do outside the office in your personal time is none of my business. However, it becomes a concern for me, if your, let's say, 'reckless' lifestyle starts affecting your performance at work."

Vikram said nothing. He just waited, staring at Dev's face. Dev was trying to come across as an open-minded person, which, Vikram knew very well, he was not.

"And now I'm told that Manvi has left you. Your personal life is a mess, really. I'm not sure how *that's* going to impact your work," Dev added.

"Dev, who told you? I mean, how did you come to know about Manvi?" Vikram finally spat out the question that had been bothering him.

Dev showed a hint of irritation. "Why is *that* so important? I told you, Vikram, we are all friends here."

"That's important for *me*, Dev. I have every right to find out who's been bitching about me behind my back." For a split second, Vikram glanced at Ashwin. Ashwin's face was flushed. He avoided Vikram's eyes and turned to face Dev. Vikram got his answer.

Dev did not answer Vikram's question. He said, "Vikram, I have a lot of respect for you as a professional, as does everybody in the firm. Your success is really vital for the future of this company. You know it and I know it. I want all of us to give our best at work."

"And what makes you think that I'm not giving my best at work?" Vikram retorted.

"Results, Vikram, results! They don't seem to be speaking in your favour. And we all know why," Dev's voice betrayed his resentment. He did not like being challenged. Over the years, as NexGen had grown in wealth and success, Dev had got accustomed to reverence and unquestioned acquiescence from those around him.

Something snapped inside Vikram.

"Dev, what you don't know is… *this*," he fished out his phone from his pocket and his fingers played around on the screen till he pulled up the pictures of Ashwin with Manvi.

"How do you think I'll be at peace when my *friend* is hell bent, not only on screwing me at work, but is also taking my wife out on secret lunch dates and filling her with crap about me?" He thrust the phone within inches of Dev's eyes, turning it to Ashwin the very next moment. "Mind explaining, *buddy*?"

Ashwin swallowed hard. He had clearly not seen it coming.

"Vikram, listen… I can explain this," Vikram sensed a slight hesitation in Ashwin's voice. "Manvi was worried. She had been receiving mysterious calls from a woman. About you…"

"And instead of asking me, she asked *you*?"

"Yes, she did. As she wasn't so sure that you'd be completely honest with her. Those calls were freaking her out!" Ashwin raised his voice a couple of notches. "Vikram, you can stay in denial for the rest of your life. But, the fact is that, Manvi doesn't trust you. And when she needed facts, she got in touch with me."

"Listen, Ashwin… Manvi tried to bullshit me with the same story. Save it for a fucking idiot, do you two get it? I'm not one," Vikram shouted, almost lunging at Ashwin.

"And who the hell took those pictures? Have you set a detective on me, Vikram? How dare you!" Ashwin's face was within inches of Vikram's.

"Boys!" Dev took a deep breath and pulled Vikram and Ashwin apart. "Look at me. Let's not digress here, okay? You two can fight this out on the street if you want to. But, I've no interest on who's dating whom, and who's getting prank calls on the phone! Am I clear?"

Vikram and Ashwin glared at each other.

"I'm talking to you, Vikram. Because I hope that you will sort out your issues at home, stop living on the edge, stop dating girls from the office, and go back to doing great work that we all want you to do, and know that you can do, if you put your heart to it. And I want the two of you to work together like civilized adults. Whatever happened between the two of you should remain your private business. We work together for the company, take it to new heights, and we make a lot of money. Isn't that what we all want?"

For a moment, the idea of a life and an office without the stress he was currently dealing with seemed to comfort Vikram. But he knew that was not to be. His life was too messed up for that.

"That's what we all want, indeed," Vikram said.

"Good." Dev smiled.

"Just that things won't play out the way you said just now, Dev."

"Why not, Vikram?"

Answers flashed through Vikram's mind. Because Ashwin is a snake. Because Ashwin is eyeing my chair. Because Ashwin will do anything to get my job. Because Ashwin is probably fucking my wife, trying to mess up my home. Because Ashwin is a liar. Because I have no respect for Ashwin. Because Ashwin has no respect for me. Because you are ready to believe anything that Ashwin says. Because no one trusts me anymore. Because…

"Things have gone too far," Vikram managed to say.

Dev stared at him and said, "They can be made to go back, Vikram."

"I don't think so," Vikram looked at Dev in the eyes.

The colour rose to Dev's face. He leaned forward and said almost in whispers, "Listen, Vikram. Let me be very clear. I gave you this job. I believed in you. I gave you your start, I gave you all the help you needed, and I created opportunities for you. And I expect you to excel at what you do for NexGen, for me. By fixing whatever is wrong with your life. Do you get that?" Dev stood up. "I've given my blood and sweat to NexGen and I'll not let you destroy my dream," Dev walked out of the booth, pushing angrily past Ashwin.

Ashwin stayed back for a couple of seconds, glaring at Vikram, and then ran after his boss.

"First Manvi and now Dev!" Vikram thumped the table in front of him. "Well done, Ashwin!"

31

TWO WEEKS LATER

Vikram felt groggy as he moved the sheets off his bare body and reached for the nagging alarm clock. He wished he could go back to sleep for a couple more hours. But that was the last thing he could afford.

If there was one thing he did not look forward to that morning, it was his meeting with Dev at nine. He knew he was already late. Yet, he was struggling to pull himself out of bed.

The phone rang. It was Dev.

"Where exactly are you?" Dev was uncharacteristically curt. And that always meant trouble.

"Getting ready, Dev. I'll be out in a couple of minutes," Vikram removed the covers and sprang out of bed. He was already heading towards the shower.

"Switch on the goddamned TV, Vikram! And head for whichever is your favourite business channel, unless you prefer watching porn over your breakfast!"

Something was wrong, very wrong.

For a split second, Vikram could not make up his mind whether he should head for the shower or the living room. He decided in favour of the living room. If the business channels were indeed up to something, he had to find out, and help Dev calm down. Dev was going ballistic at the other end of the line.

Vikram slumped into the sofa in front of the television with a glass of orange juice, and switched on the television, heading straight for Business 24x7. What he saw blew him away.

A correspondent was reporting a press meet from Tokyo. The bulletin said that Alpha Tech had announced in Tokyo that very morning a new range of smartphones and wearable devices with extraordinary features and designs. The features that were being played out in the form of an animation in the bulletin were an exact replica of what Rakesh had been working on for months.

Vikram could feel a cold wave course down his spine, as the glass almost slipped from his hand. He knew NexGen was not yet ready with the first lot they were producing in collaboration with Quantum. He had spoken with the team in Tokyo just the day before.

Vikram thrust his head back on the sofa and closed his eyes. Dev was still going on at the other end of the line, blaming Rakesh and him for their 'carelessness' and 'unprofessionalism', even hinting at 'foul play' and threatening Vikram with 'dire consequences' if any of Dev's 'suspicions was proved right'.

The world around Vikram was reduced to a blur as the walls in the room seemed to close in on him from all sides.

32

Rakesh and Vikram sat across the table from Dev. Dev's eyes bored into them alternately. The coffee on the table had gone cold.

Rakesh looked distraught. His hair was in a mess. He had not had the time to shave. His shirt was untucked. He had rushed to office as soon as he had received Vikram's call.

"There is no other way the designs could have reached Alpha! Must be the guys at Quantum. I've been apprehensive all along and, —" Rakesh could not finish.

Dev raised a hand shutting him up, and then stood up from his chair. With his arms folded behind him, he paced up and down the spacious conference room with his brow creased, considering the possibility Rakesh had suggested. He then stopped in his tracks and turned towards Vikram and Rakesh.

"So, you're sure it's our partner who's at fault? And we should start the investigations in Japan? Very convenient, isn't it? Do you mind offering me one good reason why I should believe you?" He thumped on the desk. "Quantum has been losing ground to Alpha steadily over the last several quarters in the Japanese market. They are fierce competitors! Why on earth would Quantum pass on our designs to Alpha?"

He looked at Vikram.

"Vikram, why should I consider this mere coincidence that we lost to Alpha here in Mumbai the deal with Evita which I had entrusted *you* to drive, and now, Alpha in Japan comes up with a copy of designs made by someone in *your* team, who was in Japan to collaborate with Quantum on the development of these products?" Dev glared at Vikram, who looked away.

Dev inched menacingly close to the two men in the room. "I'm giving you guys a day's time! You better show me solid evidence to support your cock-and-bull story! Or, come up with a more believable one. Let me make this very clear, guys – your jobs are on the line here."

Dev was interrupted by a knock on the glass door. It was Nancy, the office receptionist.

Dev cast an angry glance at her. "Anything urgent, Nancy?" he fumed.

"My apologies, sir," she turned to Vikram and continued, "Mr Oberoi, it's your wife. She's at the reception and says she needs to see you immediately." Nancy muttered, hesitantly. Vikram was not sure he had heard Nancy right.

"My wife? Manvi?" Vikram asked.

"Yes, Mr Oberoi. It's Manvi ma'am," Nancy replied.

"What in god's name is she doing in the office?" Vikram blurted out.

Nancy looked alternately at Dev and Vikram, finally fixing her eyes on Vikram. "Sir, I'm really sorry to barge in like this, but she would not listen. She said it's very urgent and… and she wanted to see you immediately."

Nancy sounded apologetic.

"Dev, I'll be back in a bit," Vikram stood up to leave. Dev glared at his receding figure.

As Vikram walked down the corridor on his way to the reception area, with rows of cubicles on both sides, he realized that all eyes were fixed on him. He had no idea why. He looked questioningly at Nancy who walked next to him, hoping she would help him understand what was going on. But Nancy maintained her distance. She avoided Vikram's eyes and looked away.

As he passed the last cubicle before the glass door that opened to the reception area, where Manvi was supposed to be waiting for him, his eyes went to the computer screen of the girl who was sitting in that cubicle.

And he saw himself on the screen. Naked. With a girl. Naked, too.

33

Vikram changed course and walked briskly in the direction of the computer screen. The girl sitting in that cubicle tried to say something, but her words did not reach his ears.

He studied the screen carefully. The video was on YouTube, and the whole office was watching it; the whole city, and the whole world for that matter. Vikram's eyes went to the title of the clip. It read:

NEXGEN BOSS CAUGHT ON CAMERA WITH PANTS DOWN – UNCUT VERSION

Vikram looked closer at the video. And it all came back in a flash.

He remembered the girl. She had introduced herself in Poison as Kaamna. The place where the drama was unfolding on the computer screen in front of him was his penthouse in Prestige Apartments.

Vikram remembered he was too drunk.

And the girl had filmed all of it!

And she had chosen that very day to upload her masterpiece on YouTube!

Why did she do that? That was the question uppermost in Vikram's mind.

Vikram looked up. Manvi had stormed in from the reception through the glass door without waiting for him to step out.

It seemed as if the air had been sucked out of his lungs in a split second as Manvi's kick landed on Vikram's crotch, accompanied by a collective sigh from the entire staff on the floor, now on its feet.

Vikram doubled up, his face contorted in pain.

As he managed to look up, he saw Manvi walking away. She stopped in her tracks, turned around, flashed her middle finger at Vikram and kept walking.

When he looked up again, Vikram saw Dev towering over him. Vikram looked sideways at the nearest computer screen and saw the girl who had called herself Kaamna, squirming in his arms, and her bare back to the camera. Dev was looking at the same spectacle. He shook his head in dismay.

"Disgusting!" Dev screamed.

He brought his face very close to Vikram's and said, "Vikram, I wish we were not in the office and I could have expressed myself better. I'm having a tough time here trying to restrain myself. All I can say now is – leave my office! Now! And don't ever come back!"

❖

In the meantime, Rakesh had come out of the meeting room, following Dev. His eyes went to a computer screen where the lewd action was playing out. He stepped closer and his eyes squinted. Wasn't this the same girl he had slept with in Tokyo? His heart sank and the colour vanished from his face.

Rakesh could now smell a sinister plot, connecting the theft of his designs in Tokyo, and now, the YouTube video that would, beyond doubt, cost Vikram his job. It was the same girl!

Rakesh was about to call out to Dev and break the news. That was when the realization dawned on him. What was he going to tell Dev? He had everything to lose if he went ahead and made a confession about his rendezvous with that girl inside his hotel room in Tokyo. It was in his best interest to keep mum.

34

Agastya barely moved out of the designated room for the Systems and Network team, barring his occasional visits to the cafeteria to fetch his soda and takeaway food. The hubbub on the floor outside his room had piqued his curiosity and he sent one of the trainees in his team to go find out what the buzz in the office was all about. He hoped it was not another virus attack.

"Agastya, you don't want to miss this," the trainee returned in a flash and almost ran to Agastya's seat, his excitement palpable. With a few clicks, he opened up YouTube in Agastya's laptop, and then with a few frenzied key strokes, pulled up a video.

Agastya's first reaction was to turn his face away from the sordid scene on his laptop screen, and to give the boy a piece of his mind, reminding him about office policies that prohibited watching porn at work. And then his eyes went to the girl on the screen, in the arms of – Vikram Oberoi, of all people!

He looked closer and his jaw dropped. That was Ruchika! The girl he had been planning to call up just a while back to find out when they could go on a weekend date to Lonavala that he had been planning for a while. The girl he had fallen in love with, for the very first time in his life! The one who was his comrade in his battle against the scamsters in NexGen!

Everyone from his team was now huddled around his chair, devouring the shameless antics of the boss and the girl of Agastya's dreams.

Agastya's eyes stung. He was afraid he would start crying. He pushed the chair back and stood up. He mumbled a feeble "Excuse me…" and headed for the door. He wondered if that romp playing out on his laptop screen also had anything to do with the investigations. He had to call Ruchika to find out!

"Back to work, all of you!" He managed to holler as he walked out, his voice shaking. He pulled up Ruchika's number from his list of contacts and called her. As he pressed the phone to his ear with a sweaty hand, he was told that the number was unavailable.

35

Vikram watched the video one more time inside his car parked in the basement of his office. He then threw the phone on the dashboard and turned the ignition on, when he heard a rap on the window and looked up.

It was Agastya. Vikram lowered the glass, and before he could say anything, Agastya asked him, "Sir, do you have a few minutes?"

"I'm in a hurry, Agastya. Anything urgent?" Vikram wished he could tell him that he did not have his job, and even if Agastya had to say that NexGen was faced with the worst cyber-attack in the history of mankind, it would not matter to him anymore.

"I won't take a lot of time, sir," Agastya almost pleaded with Vikram. "Just a few minutes, but I need to tell you something really important."

"Okay, come in. And whatever you have to say Agastya, it better be worth my time!"

Agastya entered the car and sat down next to Vikram. Vikram turned the air conditioner on.

"What is it, Agastya?"

"It's about that – that video…" Agastya pointed towards Vikram's phone on the dashboard.

"Okay… what – what about it?" Vikram's face was flushed and he could feel his ears burning.

"I… I know that girl," Agastya blurted out the words, his head bowed.

Vikram sat up straight, his eyes fixed on Agastya.

"What do you mean you *know* that girl? She's a bloody hooker!"

Agastya kept quiet and then he looked up at Vikram.

"Sir, I think we've been taken for a ride…"

"You said '*we*'! What's *that* supposed to mean?" Vikram's eyes narrowed.

Agastya could not meet Vikram's eyes. "I've been in a dilemma all this while… ever since I saw the video. I couldn't make up my mind whether I should share this with you. And then, I decided I should. I… I don't care what you would think of me…"

"Come on Agastya, cut the crap and come to the point, will you?" Vikram sounded impatient.

"That girl… her name is 'Ruchika'…"

"I see. She was 'Kaamna' when she met *me*. She must be having a dozen other names…"

"I was told that she worked for an agency investigating into a scam involving NexGen…"

"An investigation agency? A scam involving NexGen? Who told you *that*?"

"I received a call... from a guy... a few months back... and then she got in touch with me..."

"Why the fuck did you not tell me *then*?" Vikram could feel his rage boiling inside him.

"I was told that it was a covert operation... that I wasn't supposed to discuss this with anyone in the firm... not even with my boss... as everyone was a suspect..."

"And you believed them? How could you be such an ass, Agastya?"

Agastya swallowed hard. "I met Ruchika... she even showed me an ID... they offered money... and they were very regular with payments... it was a lot of money, Vikram... I couldn't find a single reason to doubt them..."

"You fucking moron!" Vikram thumped his fist on the dashboard. "And what did they want from you?"

"They wanted information... passwords to Admin accounts... copies of emails..."

"Copies of emails? My emails too?" Vikram could not believe his ears.

"Yes... Yes, sir," Agastya mumbled, "I'm sorry..."

Vikram pounced on Agastya and held him by his collars. "You son of a bitch! You gave them copies of my emails in exchange for money?"

Agastya's face was flushed. He was sweating profusely, even though the air conditioner was on full blast.

Vikram let go of Agastya's collars and banged his own head against the steering wheel. Then, he realized something and sat up straight.

"When was this? Was it before the last time we spoke in my cabin? Was it before we had lost the partnership deal with Evita?"

"Y-yes, sir…" Agastya's eyes had welled up, "I… I'm sorry, sir… I believed them…"

"You fucking idiot! Do you have any idea what you have done to this firm… to me?" Vikram shouted. "And who did you give those details to? To that hooker in the video? Ruchika, or, Kaamna, or whatever?"

"Y-yes, sir."

"It wasn't just the money, was it? She fucked you as well, didn't she?"

Agastya kept quiet.

"Tell me, you son of a bitch! Did she fuck you?"

Agastya nodded without looking at Vikram.

Vikram threw his head back and talked almost in whispers, "So *someone* pays you a lot of money… gets a girl to seduce you… and sucks off confidential company information which you have access to… and we end up losing the Evita deal. Then, the same girl seduces me… fucks my brains out… makes a video… puts it up on the Internet… and here I am… thrown out of my job… now, who the hell is that *someone*?"

Vikram turned to Agastya again.

"When was the last time this girl contacted you?"

"More than a month back… I haven't heard from her since then…"

"And what did she ask you to do then?"

"She wanted to know the password for the Admin account of Rakesh sir's laptop… Rakesh sir was about to travel to Japan…

and she said that the agency suspected that he was travelling to close some shady overseas deals for the company… and… and that, they would need to secretly check his laptop for any information that would help them build a case against him…"

Vikram closed his eyes, as the implication of that piece of information took its own time to sink in.

He reached for his phone and pulled up Rakesh Behl's number.

36

Rakesh took his time to make up his mind and took Vikram's call after four or five rings.

"Hi… Hi Vikram," his voice was already shaky.

"Rakesh, I want you to be honest with me… can you promise me that you'd be?" Vikram cut to the chase. There was no time for pleasantries.

"What are you talking about, Vikram?"

"Rakesh, what happened in Tokyo?"

"What… what do you mean?"

"Did you spend time with anyone… anyone who didn't belong either to NexGen or Quantum… anyone who might have had access to your laptop… and all the designs and plans you were carrying with you for the workshop with Quantum?"

"No, Vikram. I didn't meet anyone I didn't know, who'd have anything to do with our product designs and plans…"

"Rakesh, think hard. Anyone at all?" Vikram hesitated for a moment and then said, "Anyone you might have invited to your room in the hotel?"

"Vikram, what's *that* supposed to mean?"

Vikram lost his composure. The veneer of decency he had been struggling to maintain with Rakesh finally slipped off.

"Rakesh, for god's sake! Tell me the truth! You know very well what that's supposed to mean. Did you bring someone to your room? Someone who had enough time to steal information from your laptop? Listen, I'm trying to find out facts. And I swear I'm not going to hold this against you. You know, I don't have the fucking job anymore and I give a rat's ass to what happens to NexGen. But I'm going to find out who brought this on all of us! And there's going to be no mercy for that bastard. So… will you help me, or you won't?"

The line went quiet at the other end.

Vikram realized that Rakesh was thinking. He said, "Rakesh, look… I've already found out that someone's been playing games with me, with NexGen. I've figured out how we ended up losing Evita. And how I lost my job today. I want to find out if it's the same bastard who's responsible for the debacle in Tokyo."

"Vikram, promise me you'll keep this to yourself," Rakesh finally spoke.

"You have my word for it, Rakesh."

"I… I did meet a girl… in the flight from Mumbai… she travelled with me to Tokyo. We put up in the same hotel, had dinner together… a few drinks… and then, went up to my room… and… and we spent the night together…"

"Go on, Rakesh. I'm listening."

"She said she worked for a travel magazine and had an assignment in Tokyo, and she left in the morning."

"Your laptop was in your room. Was she alone inside your room at any time?"

"Yyes… she was, Vikram… I was in the shower. Also, she could have gotten up anytime during the night while I was asleep…"

"And did you meet her after that morning?"

"No… Amyra said she would be out completing her assignment and flying back the same evening… even joked about the shoestring budgets that her magazine had, said she would have loved to spend more time with me…"

"Rakesh, I hate to ask you this, but – but have you seen the goddamned video that has cost me my job?"

"Y…yes, Vikram… I have," Rakesh paused briefly, a slight hesitation in his voice. And then he said, "I know what you're going to ask next, Vikram. It *was* the same girl… the girl in the video is the one who was with me in Tokyo… Amyra…"

"Great!" Vikram thumped the steering wheel with his hand, "Amyra! That's the third name I'm hearing."

"What do you mean?"

"The same girl used two other names on two different occasions, Rakesh."

"Vikram, do you think she's the one who stole the designs and the plans from my laptop?"

"I don't *think*, buddy! I *know* she's the one!"

"But how the hell did she manage to get into my laptop?"

"This is a conspiracy, Rakesh. These assholes had your password!"

37

Vikram lost count of the number of reporters who kept calling him on his phone. He finally switched it off and threw it on the dashboard of his car as he turned the bend of the road leading to his house.

He could see from a distance the crowd of reporters, cameras, and vans around the entrance to his bungalow. They reminded him of vultures waiting to pounce on a carcass. There was no way he would be able to make his way through those gates for the next few days.

He made a U-turn and headed for his private penthouse in Prestige Apartments. It was unlikely the reporters and the paparazzi would know about it.

He smiled at his fate. Vikram Oberoi was now a man on the run!

Vikram did not know that his worst nightmare was just getting started.

38

The penthouse did seem like a safe haven away from the nosey reporters and press photographers.

The events of the day sat heavy on Vikram. He poured himself a large Macallan. He switched on his phone, and called Sonal, but she did not pick up.

He needed to get his thoughts together and draw up an action plan. The very first thing he needed to do was to call up his lawyer. The video on the Internet had to be brought down immediately. He had no clue how, though. His lawyer would take care of that, although the damage must have already been done. The girl, who had used different names on different occasions, was surely a pawn. Vikram had to figure out who was the mastermind behind this.

He picked up the remote and turned the television on. He switched channels to the evening news bulletin. Vikram sat up straight as his eyes went to the ticker at the bottom of the screen.

WOMAN ACCUSES NEXGEN BOSS OF SEXUAL HARASSMENT

Vikram finished off the whiskey in one swig and cranked up the volume of the television.

They were airing an 'exclusive' interview. The newsreader was in the studio asking questions. There was the pixelated face of a woman occupying a third of the television screen, answering her. The word 'Recorded' flashed in the top-left corner of the screen.

The interviewer appreciated the courage of the woman. Not only had she decided to open up, but she had also agreed to appear on national television in person to share her sensational story.

Vikram could never go wrong with the voice from the television that filled the room.

The girl was Sonal Verma.

39

As Vikram drained another glass of whisky, his shock having taken the better of him, he could only register bits and pieces of the conversation on the television that blared in the closed room.

Sonal was recounting how for months, Vikram Oberoi had been sexually exploiting her with promises of promotion and higher salary in the office.

"I've been afraid of hostile consequences all these months. What if I didn't play along?" Sonal sniffled.

"Ma'am, would you be able to prove your allegations in a court? Cases like this often fizzle out for lack of adequate evidence."

"I would be able to produce evidence in a court of law to support all my allegations. *I have videos*."

"Ma'am, you claim that you have evidence to support your allegations in a court of law. But still, you've been going through hell for the last several months. You say that you've been afraid of consequences. What made you change your mind and open up *today*?"

Vikram took another long swig. He had the same question.

"You know what hurts the most? It's betrayal. Over the last couple of weeks, I had started believing Mr Oberoi. Maybe his promises were true, after all. Maybe he was genuinely in love with me. Maybe we have a future together. I even toyed with the idea of deleting for good, the videos I had made some time back out of sheer desperation and helplessness," Sonal paused.

"And then?" The interviewer was trying her best to sound sympathetic, while continuing to probe Sonal mercilessly.

"And then, the video surfaced on the Internet today."

"You mean the one on YouTube, where Mr Vikram Oberoi is seen with an unknown woman in a compromising position?" The interviewer made sure that she meticulously described the embarrassing video in so many words.

"Yes… yes, that one. You know, that was my birthday," more sniffling. "How could a man in love with a woman have sex with someone else on her birthday? That broke me completely. It flipped a switch inside. I told myself, 'This is it! I cannot let this monster of a man get away with this!' That's when I decided to come out with my story…"

Vikram gulped hard!

There was not going to be any room for favourable judgements after his lewd video that had gone online, followed by this revelation from Sonal. Vikram was well aware of the penalties of sexual exploitation of a person in a subordinate position, abuse, and aggravated abuse. He had no idea what all that sick bitch had filmed secretly. Sometimes, their acts in that very penthouse had got really violent in the throes of passion. Those could easily be construed as acts of violence on a helpless victim of sexual assault.

If Sonal's evidences went to the police, or god forbid, ended up in the hands of the media, his career and his life – whatever little was left of them after the events of the last few hours – would be over.

And once again, that fatal blow had been brought on him by the disgusting video, which had made Sonal change her mind and open up before the world about their clandestine affair. If only he could figure out who had hatched the masterplan. And had set the hooker on him. And on Agastya, and on Rakesh.

Barely able to stand straight, Vikram poured himself another drink. Sonal's words kept playing in his mind. There was something she had said just now that was bothering him. Something that was not adding up. He could not put his finger on it, but it bugged him at the back of his mind.

Suddenly, Vikram sat up straight.

He picked up his mobile phone from the coffee table, and went to YouTube. He had lost count of the number of times he had already seen the video. But, he wanted to see it one more time. All of it. Just to be sure.

And when he finished playing the video, he knew what had been bothering him all this while.

Nowhere in the video was there any mention of the date when it had been shot.

How did Sonal Verma know that it was her birthday?

40

Vikram sat staring at the ceiling in drunken stupor. But his mind raced.

He considered several possibilities. He finally realized that there could be only one answer to that question.

It was Sonal Verma who had set the hooker on him that night. And on Agastya. And on Rakesh. She was the mastermind behind the conspiracy.

Vikram was finding it difficult to believe that Sonal had been playing him all these months. That she was the woman who had been systematically carrying out her evil plans leading to his downfall – on all fronts.

And she was the woman with whom Vikram had been planning to spend the rest of his life! The woman for whom he was ready to throw away everything that had ever mattered to him!

Everything was now beginning to fall in place.

Sonal had been using her position in NexGen to the hilt. She was the one making lunch and dinner reservations for Ashwin's meetings with Evita, and must have got wind of the deal. And then, Agastya had been lured with money and sex. She had gained access to the details of the Evita proposal and passed it on to Alpha, who had created a similar proposal with a few additional benefits, which had made Evita decide in their favour.

She was the one who had made the travel arrangements for Rakesh's trip to Tokyo, and must have got to know from him what the trip was about. The girl, who had earlier seduced Agastya and him, had once again been called to action. She had robbed Rakesh of the product designs and plans and handed them over to Alpha in Japan.

And then, the allegation of sexual exploitation against Vikram! Sonal had enticed him and provoked him to get into a sexual relationship, all the while recording damning evidence. She had also made sure that his image had been adequately tainted *before* she went public with the harassment allegations, thanks to that lewd video on the Internet, which she now described as the trigger for her confessions.

Although Vikram still had a nagging doubt if Sonal had been working alone. The more important question that loomed large before Vikram, though, was 'why'.

41

His phone rang. It was Aarti.

"Vikram, I'd never have called you… but I'm watching the news right now," she slurred on the phone, heavily drunk, "and I couldn't stop myself from calling you one last time. Serves you right, you sick son of a—" she laughed hysterically and then continued, "I can't believe I fell in love with *you*... and I was ready to do anything to get *you* back... I was out of my mind..."

"Aarti, we can fix this together. It's a fucking conspiracy. I need your help, sweetheart. Leaving you for that bitch was a mistake. You know how much—" Drunk beyond his wits himself, Vikram made a feeble attempt at getting Aarti back on his side.

"Shut the fuck up, Vikram!" Aarti screamed at the other end of the line. "And just so you know, I applied for a job at Alpha sometime back, and they've already made an offer… I've been in touch with Arun Sundaram and will be working for him from next week… you can go to hell…" Arun had offered Aarti a position in Alpha and had made sure that she was happy with her compensation. Aarti had accepted the offer after a final discussion with Arun Sundaram the same night as Evita's announcement of the partnership with Alpha during the fashion show at Majestic.

Vikram shifted in his chair as Aarti went on, "Oh and one last thing… tell your wife she sounds lovely over the phone… of course, if she cares to see your face ever again!"

"Aarti, you fucking bitch! So you're the one who's been calling Manvi all these days… bitching about me? But… but how did you manage to find out where and with whom I've been spending my evenings? Have you been stalking me?"

Aarti did not let Vikram finish. Amid bouts of hysterical laughter, she said, "No Vikram. I haven't been stalking you, if that's what you are thinking. I hired someone for the job. Does the name 'Albert Pinto' ring a bell?"

"Albert?" Vikram could not believe what he had just heard.

"Yes, Vikram. Albert. You used to hire him for running secret background checks on new recruits. You told me about him many moons ago when we were together. You probably don't even remember!"

"Aarti, you bitch—"

The line went dead.

Sonal, in the meantime, was going on with her interview on the television. Her words seemed to be wafting in from the far end of a long, dark tunnel, Vikram registering only bits and pieces.

When his phone buzzed, Vikram picked it up from the table in front of him. There was a text.

From Sonal.

Vikram squinted his eyes and opened the message. It read:

"Remember Rishi Bhargav?"

Vikram suddenly felt numb, sitting on his sofa in front of the television, as he finished yet another drink, vacillating between panic and intoxication.

The coin dropped.

The 'why' was answered.

42

SOMETIME LAST YEAR

Sonal Verma and Rishi Bhargav went to the same school and were in the same class. They were best friends all through their school days, who sat next to each other, shared tiffin and comics, and when one fell sick and missed school, the other made two copies of class notes. Rishi was better at studies and Sonal prayed for him to top the class in every examination. Sonal was better on the field and the loudest cheers came from Rishi every time she ran in the annual sports.

They were in their first year in college, when they discovered their love for each other.

And it all started under rather extraordinary circumstances.

It was a lazy Sunday afternoon and they had met up at the Inorbit Mall in Malad. Sonal was trying very hard to walk gracefully in her new four-inch heels which she had coaxed her father to get her for her birthday. She was conscious of men and women staring at her as she tottered in those heels.

"Rishi, do you think I'm making a complete fool of myself?" Sonal whispered in Rishi's ears with some trepidation.

"No way, Soni! You look totally sexy." Rishi smiled reassuringly, as Sonal clutched his arm.

"You know what, the last time I had worn these darned things – it was a wedding – I had actually ended up twisting my ankle. Just imagine, Rishi! The *baraat* was just coming in and I went—" Sonal dropped to the ground on her knees with a pain-stricken "Ouch!"

Rishi turned around.

"I don't believe this, *nautanki*!" he smiled, "You're actually acting it out, inside a shopping mall? What the—"

Sonal's face was contorted in pain. "I'm not acting, duffer! I've actually twisted my ankle… again!"

Rishi extended his hand. "Damn! Really? Can you get up?"

"I… I can't Rishi!"

The colour drained off Rishi's face and his heart skipped several beats, when Sonal looked into his eyes, tears streaming down her cheeks. Rishi got down on his knees. He got Sonal to throw an arm around his shoulders and he scooped her up from the ground. He stood up carrying Sonal in his arms, and said, "Don't worry, Soni. I'll handle this."

Sonal kept looking at his face wide-eyed, as Rishi cradled her in his arms and made his way through the afternoon crowd inside Inorbit towards a medical store. He picked up a crepe bandage and carried her in his arms out of the shopping area to the steps outside. As Sonal sat up straight, her back against the wall, Rishi sat at her feet, and wrapped the bandage around her ankle.

"Here, have some water and breathe easy," Rishi handed her a bottle of Bisleri, "and wait here for me."

Rishi rushed back into the mall. This time, to the Hush Puppies store on the ground floor, and picked up a pair of flat slippers for Sonal. Returning to where he had left Sonal, he took off her heels, cursing them profusely, and then slid her feet into the new pair of slippers.

"See if you can walk now."

Sonal stood up with a lot of difficulty and put an arm around Rishi's shoulders. As soon as she tried to take a step forward, the pain made her grimace.

Rishi picked her up in his arms again and walked towards the exit of the mall. Sonal rested her head on Rishi's chest, right next to his heart. She realized that all eyes were fixed on them – girls who turned green in envy and nudged their boyfriends in the ribs; boys who cursed Rishi silently for setting this unbelievable caring-boyfriend goal!

As she nuzzled her face on Rishi's chest, Sonal realized that the only other man who had ever carried her around in his arms in public was her father when she was still in her diapers. She had not noticed when her tears had dried away, and a smile had appeared at the corner of her lips, even as her foot hurt like hell!

When they got into a cab, Rishi's arm was still around her. Her head rested on his shoulder. And that was where it stayed through their ride back home, as the wind played with Sonal's hair, tossing it up all over Rishi's face, not a word exchanged between them.

❖

The next few months turned out to be the best of their lives.

Sonal and Rishi skipped classes and left college early to spend their evenings together, mostly in D'Souza Uncle's coffee shop near the campus. The table in one corner had become theirs by an unwritten agreement with D'Souza Uncle, who had to literally pull the shutters down at ten in the night to get Sonal and Rishi out. They were inseparable during the weekends. They had not realized earlier that there was so much to talk about all through the night on the phone, till they dozed off. Rishi usually was the first to start snoring.

Sonal's eyes searched for Rishi the moment she stepped into the campus. She felt jealous when Rishi talked with other girls. Every time it rained and the earth smelt sweet, she texted Rishi to tell him that she was thinking of him, and then waited impatiently for his reply. These were emotions Sonal had never felt before, and she had never imagined, in the wildest of her dreams, that she ever would, of all men, with Rishi!

They were in love and life had never been better.

Sonal snuggled closer to Rishi as soon as the lights in the auditorium went off. Like always, Rishi passed an arm around her and pulled her closer. As the movie started, Sonal rested her head on Rishi's chest. Sonal loved the sound of his heartbeats, which she knew were for her.

The warmth of her breath on him sent Rishi's pulse racing. He kissed her on her head. And she raised her face, her eyes meeting his in the darkness.

They kissed – for the first time. Through the entire length of the song they had been humming together over the last few days, while walking back from D'Souza Uncle's coffee shop late in the evenings, along the lonely lanes and by-lanes, their fingers locked.

Sonal had no idea that a kiss could make one giddy and make one lose sense of time and place. As her heart pounded against her ribs, Sonal could feel their souls talking. She felt complete and contented down to the very core of her being, like she had never felt before. She realized how much she loved Rishi. She wanted him to be hers for the rest of her life.

43

It was around three in the afternoon. Sonal looked at her watch and wondered if Rishi would be able to make it. There were campus interviews going on for Engineering students, and Rishi had not been able to join her for lunch for the past couple of days. She was sitting alone at the corner table in D'Souza Uncle's coffee shop and was beginning to get conscious of a bunch of boys sitting a couple of tables away, who were stealing glances at her, and talking in whispers. About her, she had no doubt.

That was when she saw Rishi. He waved at her, then flashed a 'V' and then ran across the road into the coffee shop, beaming.

"What is this, Rishi? You should never keep a lady waiting for so long!" D'Souza Uncle smiled at him.

"D'Souza Uncle, just keep watching! The lady will jump in joy when I give her the good news!" Rishi said without looking back, making his way to the table, "A pizza for us. With extra cheese! We're having a party!"

"Soniiii!" Rishi screamed and took Sonal in a tight hug when he reached the table and let her go only when she was gasping for breath.

"Phew, Rishi! What the hell is wrong with you?"

"Wrong? On the contrary, everything's beginning to fall in place, Miss Verma!" Rishi flashed the sheet of paper he was carrying, "What do you think *this* is? Make a guess!"

"Rishi, is it what I think it is? You – you've got a job?" Sonal's eyes were already wide.

"The worst part about having a smart girlfriend is that you can never give her a surprise!" Rishi made a sad face for a fleeting second before he was back to his loud, jovial self. "Yes, darling, your boyfriend now has a job! In NexGen!"

Some of the regulars who had been sitting around them and listening to the conversation started clapping. Rishi stood up dramatically on a chair and bowed. Sonal kept clapping as her eyes welled up, her face lit up by her smile. Rishi climbed down and hugged her again, as Uncle D'Souza served them their pizza and chocolate shakes.

"Today's lunch is on me, Rishi! God bless both of you," he made a cross on his chest. Rishi hugged him tight.

After Rishi had settled down and taken the first bite of the pizza, Sonal took his hand in hers and said, "Rishi, I'm so proud of you! NexGen is *the* company everyone is talking about. How many offers did they make in our campus?"

"Only five of us got selected. Guess what, you've a smart boyfriend!" Rishi winked.

"I never doubted that!" Sonal pecked him on the cheek.

Rishi looked at Sonal and said, "Hey, listen… I've something for you here." And he pulled out a form.

"Soni, I figured out that they are also looking for interns in their Finance and Administration departments. I picked up an application form for you from their office."

"You did?" Sonal struggled to hide her tears. She wondered what she had done to be blessed with so much love!

"Fill it up tonight and we'll drop it at their office tomorrow," Rishi was going on, but his words did not reach Sonal. She was lost in her dreams.

❖

They had dropped the application form in the office of NexGen the very next day, but Sonal had not heard back from NexGen by the time college ended after a couple of months. She had already started looking for other jobs.

Sonal and Rishi had lesser and lesser time for themselves as Rishi had to work extra hours and sometimes over weekends. But Sonal did not complain. She was happy for Rishi. For as far as she could see, they had the rest of their lives to themselves.

And then, everything changed.

44

"Come in," Manvi Oberoi responded to the light knock on the door of the Oberois' suite in the Marriott.

The shopping bags were scattered all over the king-size bed. It was a warm day and Manvi had been out shopping for far too long – even by Manvi Oberoi standards. Desperate situations, as they say, call for desperate measures. And Manvi did not know if she should call that shopping spree 'retail-therapy' or 'revenge-shopping'. All she knew was that her feet and Vikram's credit card had both had a lot of exercise all through the morning. The first hurt, the second made her feel good. Well, make that great.

Manvi was in a red off-shoulder fitted dress that clung to her body and showed off her immaculately maintained curves. As Rishi walked into the suite hoping to find Vikram, he realized that Manvi was alone.

"Vikram sir wanted these files before his meeting with the Press downstairs," Rishi held up the couple of files he carried.

"Yes, Vikram called me a while back and said you'd be here."

Vikram was going to meet the press in a conference hall downstairs in less than an hour to announce the launch of a new portable music player. Rishi, who had joined NexGen as an intern about three months back, and had worked in the project, was busy giving finishing touches to the documents with specifications that Vikram would carry to the meeting.

Rishi saw Manvi walk across the room to the cupboard, picking up a robe, probably in preparation for a shower.

She turned towards him and said, "You may want to call him and check, Rishi. He wanted you to wait for him till he came back. He said he'd be back soon." Manvi looked straight into Rishi's eyes and smiled. "Make yourself comfortable, Rishi. You may want to get something from the mini bar if you want."

"Thank you! I'd wait here, ma'am." Rishi perched on the couch. Manvi stepped into the washroom.

And it was then that Rishi realized that Manvi had not closed the door to the washroom completely and he could clearly see her in the mirror facing him, hung on a wall right opposite to the washroom, offering him a view of its interiors. He was suddenly very tense.

Manvi had her back to Rishi as she let her red dress drop from her shoulder. Even as he tried his best to look away, Rishi's eyes kept going back to the mirror.

Manvi slowly turned in the direction of the half-closed door of the washroom and bent over to push the dress down below her waist, not even bothering to look in the direction of the mirror. Rishi could see her full breasts that almost spilled off her black bra. Her hair formed a drapery around her face, which was turned towards the floor. She pushed the dress down her legs and stepped out of it. With her face still lowered, she unclasped her bra.

45

Manvi did not know what had come over her. Her pulse raced as she started laying herself bare before that boy from Vikram's office, all the while pretending she had not noticed that the washroom door had been left more than ajar. Had the boy realized that she was putting on a show for him? Manvi's heart beat so hard that she was afraid the boy would hear. Her knees felt weak. She was giddy. Her throat was dry. She had never felt a rush like this for months.

For months, she had felt ignored, insecure. Vikram never bothered to touch her in bed. And then, her confidence took a severe beating the day she found out about Vikram and his new secretary Aarti.

She remembered that evening very well. Vikram was supposed to meet Manvi at the shopping mall not very far from his office and she had been waiting for him. When he did not turn up after almost an hour, Manvi decided to drop by his office herself.

It was the Thursday before a long weekend and the office was almost deserted. The receptionist was nowhere in sight.

The security guard approached her. "Ma'am, you'd need a visitor's badge."

"And how do you suggest I might get one? The receptionist doesn't seem to be around," Manvi replied haughtily.

"Well… I can see that… but—" the guard mumbled.

"Listen, you know me, don't you? I don't need a goddamned badge to walk into my husband's office," Manvi was losing patience.

"Of course, ma'am… I know you… but I have instructions…" the guard looked helpless.

"Please open the door. I don't have the rest of the evening to stand here and argue with you."

The guard swiped his card on the door and opened it for Manvi.

As she approached Vikram's glass-walled cabin, Manvi saw that the blinds were drawn and the door was shut. She was about to knock when she heard muffled voices inside. She put her ear to the door and the sounds became clearer. She could hear heavy breathing, clothes rustling and throaty moans.

Her curiosity got the better of her and she looked inside the room through a crack in the blinds. Her jaw dropped at the scene that was being played out inside Vikram's cabin.

Vikram was with a girl who looked several years younger than him. That must be Aarti, the secretary everyone was talking about. Vikram's desk had been cleared out, and the girl was bent over that desk, her pants pulled down to her ankles, Vikram right behind her.

As she looked away, Manvi did not realize when the tears had started rolling down her cheeks. She stepped back, trying to make as little noise as she could. As if she was the one who should not get caught.

She walked briskly down the corridor, signalling the guard to open the door when she reached it. The guard looked at her in surprise as she frantically ran down the stairs without waiting for the elevator, trying to get away from Vikram's office as fast as she could.

For days thereafter, Manvi was in a state of depression. She kept wondering what could possibly have turned Vikram away from her. The obvious conclusion she arrived at was that she was not attractive anymore. And it had only been downhill from there. Her self-esteem hit rock bottom and she hated herself. The retail-therapy did not always help. Nor did the heavy drinking.

Now, when she looked into the mirror, she saw the boy's flushed face. She saw his very apparent excitement, in spite of his obvious embarrassment and hesitation. And she felt the fire surge through her veins. There was no holding back from here.

Manvi crossed every limit of inhibition and began to feel herself before the gaping eyes of the boy. She basked in the rush of the perverse pleasure that she derived from her unabashed exhibitionism and self-pleasure.

She wondered if *she* should make the first move, as the boy seemed too shy to come on to the boss' wife.

❖

Manvi finally stepped out of the washroom, unable to restrain her all-consuming desire any longer. Rishi stood up, almost in reflex, and headed for the door. Manvi stopped him in his tracks and was all over him in a flash, almost pinning him down to the couch, showering moist kisses all over the boy's face.

That was when there was a click on the door and before Rishi could gather himself or Manvi could rush back to the washroom, Vikram stormed inside.

"What the..." Vikram muttered. His jaw hung, as he took in the spectacle unfolding before his eyes. Manvi sprinted back to the washroom, and shut the door behind the two men.

Vikram stood rooted to the spot for a few seconds, glaring at Rishi; his face flushed with rage, his fist clenched. He then pounced on Rishi.

As the blows landed thick and fast on his face, Rishi did not get the chance to speak. And he did not dare fight with his boss. And somewhere deep inside, Rishi blamed himself for the unprecedented turn of events. "I should have walked out long back," he kept reminding himself amid Vikram's merciless thrashing.

But the question uppermost in Rishi's mind was how he would ever face Sonal again.

"Vikram, for god's sake, please stop! It's not… not entirely his fault," Manvi, who had, in the meantime, come out of the washroom wrapped in a bathrobe, tried to get between the two.

Vikram shoved her away. There was no stopping him.

46

"Hello, this is Vikram Oberoi," Vikram was speaking with the hotel receptionist on the phone. "Can you please send a couple of your security personnel up to my suite? There has been an… an intrusion."

Rishi sat next to Vikram on the couch, crouching and aching all over. His lips were swollen, and a side of his face was badly bruised. His hair dishevelled, his shirt untucked, his breathing laboured, his spirit dead.

Vikram was thinking fast. With half an hour left before the all-important press meeting, he had to make some quick decisions.

The last thing he wanted was to get the police involved in his matters. He had far too many skeletons in his own cupboard for comfort. On the one hand, Vikram did not want to go to the police and let the incident smear the prestige of the Oberois.

On the other, there was also his male ego at play. He struggled to come to terms with the fact that Manvi had made overtures to a lowly intern in his firm. There was no way he could let that become fodder for gossip. Manvi was a sick bitch and he would have to deal with her later, behind closed doors.

Vikram turned towards Rishi and grabbed his collars.

"Now listen to me very carefully, you horny son of a bitch! Don't show your sorry face again! Do you get it?"

Rishi's eyes were fixed on the carpet.

"And thank your stars that I'm not handing you over to the cops!"

There was a knock. Vikram opened the door and two beefy security men walked into the suit.

"What's the matter, sir?" The senior one asked Vikram.

"He misbehaved with my wife," Vikram pointed at Rishi, still slumped on the couch. "I want him to be thrown out of the hotel right now."

"How did he get inside the suite, sir? Is he someone you know?"

"Yes, he worked for me. I threw him out of my firm this morning. He came back, made an excuse, and my wife let him in while I was away."

The senior, his muscles stretching his shirt sleeve, picked Rishi up by his collar. "He's just a kid, isn't he?" He turned towards his companion and continued with a look of mock concern, "What has the world come to?"

He smacked Rishi on his face, and the searing pain shot to Rishi's head.

"Is ma'am okay, sir?"

"She is in shock, but okay otherwise."

Manvi had, in the meantime, retired to the bedroom.

"Sir, we should hand him over to the cops." One more slap right across Rishi's face. This time the companion. He did not want to be left out.

"You know what? He's too young. Just out of college." Vikram tried to sound magnanimous, "I think we should give him a chance. A police complaint for molestation will screw him up for the rest of his life."

Vikram looked at his watch. Time was running out. He picked up the papers Rishi had brought for him.

"Let's go down and throw him out of the hotel. I'm getting late for the meeting."

Vikram got into the elevator with the two security personnel, one of them almost dragging Rishi by his collar.

When they stepped out of the elevator, a few more security guards on duty rushed towards them.

"Everything okay, sir?" one of them asked Vikram and then turned to his colleagues who pushed Rishi out of the elevator, "What's the matter?"

"The asshole misbehaved with sir's wife."

"Shall we call the police?"

"No one calls the police," Vikram immediately interjected.

A couple of press photographers, who had assembled in the hotel lobby to cover the NexGen event, inched closer.

Vikram did not want the focus of the Press to deviate from the product launch. But it was too late. The reporters had already started gathering around the security men who were clearly enjoying the attention and were only too happy to oblige

Press photographers and nosey reporters. They shouted over each other to get heard in the din.

"Yes… it was an attempted rape…"

"Look at him… just out of college… used to be an intern before sir threw him out this morning…"

"Wanted to get even with his boss…"

"Sir has decided not to lodge a police complaint… he is too kind…"

Vikram watched helplessly. And then an idea struck him. Instead of ruing over the mess, he could actually use this to his advantage.

It was time he spoke to the reporters. He turned towards them and said, "The Press briefing about our new product will go on, as planned. I've always been devoted to my work. And that goes way beyond personal crises like the one I'm going through right now. My wife is in a state of shock, and I will attend to her. But not before we finish the business that has brought all of us together here.

"I'm a great believer in second chances. And the boy is too young. I don't want to mess up with his future by pressing molestation charges against him. Let destiny take its own course…"

Vikram's statements were lapped up the Press. Two security men grabbed Rishi by his arms and dragged him towards the exit.

The cameras were turned on Rishi – the failed intern, expelled by the boss, who then tried to rape the boss's wife. Vikram had successfully managed to turn Manvi's indiscretion into Rishi's heinous crime. And that was going to be the scoop of the day.

In the blinding light of flashbulbs, the security personnel kicked Rishi out of the hotel.

Rishi managed to stop a cab and tottered in. And his tears finally broke free.

47

Sonal tried Rishi's number one more time. It was switched off. Just as it had been all through the evening.

It was not unusual for Rishi to work late. Sonal remembered Rishi had mentioned that they were going to have a Press briefing for a new product launch in the afternoon. However, if Rishi could not take calls, he usually sent her a text message.

"Maybe his battery is dead. And he must be too busy..." Sonal tried to reason with herself.

"Sonu, dinner is ready," Sonal could hear her mom laying out plates on the table in the dining room.

She looked at the clock. It was almost ten.

She walked into the dining room. Her parents were already seated at the table, her father's eyes fixed on the television screen. 'The News at 10' was starting.

The newsreader was rattling off the headlines of the day. Sonal looked up when she heard 'NexGen'.

"In a shocking incident, an intern with NexGen, who had been expelled from the company earlier today, tried to molest the wife of a senior leader of the firm in an act of retaliation," the newsreader said as Sonal read the words on the screen:

NEXGEN INTERN EXPELLED, TRIES TO MOLEST WIFE OF SENIOR LEADER

The visuals showed a crowded hotel lobby, a horde of press photographers and reporters, and a couple of beefy security guards in uniform making their way through the crowd dragging a boy by his collars as cameras kept flashing. The face of the boy was blurred out.

"NexGen... isn't that the company where Rishi works?" Sonal's father looked up from the plate.

"Yes, Papa," Sonal said. Picking up the remote control, she switched over to the next news channel. The same 'breaking news' was being aired. This time, with more visuals. The cameraman had managed to get closer to the boy as he was being thrown out of the hotel.

None of the channels mentioned the name of the boy or showed his face, but when Sonal looked at the T-shirt and the red stone bracelet that the 'rogue NexGen intern' was wearing, there was a dark shadow on her face. For a few minutes, she felt numb and her heart palpitated.

Then, she pushed her plate away. She picked up her phone and dialled the land phone number of Rishi's house.

48

"Hello Sonal," Anupama Bhargav took Sonal's call. Her voice was shaking. She had asked her husband, Manoj, to switch off the television a while back.

"Aunty, is everything ok? I've been trying to reach Rishi all evening… and now, the news channels…"

Sonal could not finish. She could hear Rishi's mother sniffling at the other end of the line. Sonal had choked up herself.

"Sonal, we have no idea what's going on!"

"Aunty, where's Rishi? Why isn't he taking my calls? His phone is switched off."

"Sonal, he came home early… he had bruises… said he had slipped and fallen down the stairs… said he would be fine… went straight to his room… said he was tired and needed to sleep…"

"Aunty, I'm coming over!"

"No use, Sonal... he's sleeping... he doesn't want to see anyone... he didn't even have dinner... said he wasn't hungry... Manoj knocked on his door a while back and he let us in for a few minutes... we asked him what was going on... he told us not to believe what the news channels are reporting... my boy swore on me, and I know he won't lie... he pleaded with us to switch off the television... and went back to sleep..."

Anupama had broken down. She passed the phone to Manoj.

"Hello bete," Manoj tried to sound as comforting as the circumstances permitted. It was a difficult time for everyone.

Sonal could not speak for a few seconds and then she asked, "Uncle did Rishi leave any message for me?" Her voice betrayed her hurt.

Manoj was quiet for a few seconds. Rishi had not mentioned Sonal when he had talked to him sometime back.

"Sonal, don't worry bete. Rishi is very upset, as we all can understand. There must have been a terrible misunderstanding. These television channels will stoop to any level for their TRPs. Don't you think the police would have been at our door by now if what the channels are saying was true? I'm sure it'll be fine tomorrow. Rishi will tell us everything... just the way it happened. I'll ask him to call you. Or, better still, you can come over in the morning and we can all have breakfast together. It's too late right now for you to travel also."

Sonal kept the phone down with trembling hands.

49

It was around three in the night when Sonal got the call from Manoj Bhargav, who somehow managed to deliver the news between bouts of uncontrollable crying. Sonal could hear Anupama's wailing in the background.

They had been awakened by the sound of a heavy object falling inside Rishi's room. It was the chair that Rishi had kicked off the bed on to the floor. By the time they had managed to break into Rishi's room, the bed sheet tied around his neck had squeezed out the last breath from his body that now hung lifeless, inches above his bed.

Her phone slipped off her hands, and Sonal did not realize when the tears had started spilling out. Sonal's parents rushed into her room hearing her muffled cries, and then stayed with her till the early hours of the morning, when Sonal wanted to be left alone with her unbearable grief, each moment more nerve-wracking than the last.

The next day, Rishi was on the front page of every newspaper. He was the intern who had tried to rape the wife of Vikram Oberoi after having been expelled from the company and then, had ended his life inside his room later in the night. The dead commanded no privacy and overnight, it was alright to flash Rishi's face and his name everywhere.

There were editorials and articles in newspapers, and debates on national television on topics like 'the gradually diminishing morality of today's youth', 'the adverse influence of technology and social media', and 'the inability of youngsters to cope with failures'.

Vikram Oberoi was waxed eloquent. He was hailed as the industry champion who had been kind and considerate enough to give the misguided young man a second chance, his personal trauma notwithstanding. In a tragic turn of fate, the boy had turned down that opportunity and decided to end his life.

50

As she stepped into Rishi's room the day after his last rites had been performed, Sonal felt empty inside. She looked at the TV on the wall, the laptop still propped up on Rishi's study desk. She looked at the neat pile of books in the shelves and on his desk. Rishi had been obsessed with order and cleanliness. Sonal often teasing him saying that he had OCD.

She walked over to the desk and picked up his diary. She flipped through the pages till she reached the last entry in that diary. She checked the date, and her heart jumped to her throat. Before he ended his life, Rishi had actually written down the events of that day!

Sonal sat on the edge of the bed and started reading.

❖

Her tears spilt over as the rains pelted the windows harder and cars swooshed by on the empty street below. Over the next few hours, Sonal's grief and despair slowly gave way to unbridled rage and then, a thirst for vengeance.

All that Sonal wanted for the next few days was to put a knife right through Vikram Oberoi's heart. And then, she realized a greater truth. The only things that mattered to people like Vikram Oberoi were success, wealth and prestige. Vikram Oberoi could go to any length to make sure that the family name was not tainted, and he continued to prosper, amassing money and fame. If someone were to hit him where it hurt him the most, he could be finished off without being killed.

Three months later, luck smiled on Sonal. She finally heard back from NexGen and joined their Administration department as an intern.

51

"Good Morning, you've reached Alpha Tech. How can I help you?"

"I would like to speak to Mr Arun Sundaram," Sonal looked around herself as she spoke. She was in a public phone booth.

"Just a moment, please," Sonal heard her call being redirected as the signature tune, now made famous by the television commercials of Alpha, greeted her.

A couple of seconds later, the call was picked up by Vaibhavi, Arun's secretary.

"Good Morning, this is Arun Sundaram's office. How can I help you?"

"Good Morning, my name is Sonal Verma. I would like to meet Mr Sundaram. I wanted to make an appointment."

"May I know what this is regarding, Ms Verma?"

"It's a confidential matter that I'd like to discuss with Mr Sundaram only."

"Ma'am, I'm sorry, but I'd need to know why you want to meet Mr Sundaram."

"Listen, I'm sure Mr Sundaram wouldn't want me to discuss this with *you*."

"Ma'am, I have strict instructions. I hope you understand," Vaibhavi sounded a tad helpless, unable to decide what she should do.

"Why don't you check with him right away if he'd be interested to see me? Tell him, I work for NexGen."

Vaibhavi looked sideways at Arun Sundaram's corner office. He was inside, typing away on his laptop, looking engrossed in his work. Vaibhavi debated with herself whether it would be a good idea to disturb him.

"Ma'am, trust me... this *is* important. For me. More importantly, for *him*," Sonal sounded insistent.

"Alright, give me a couple of minutes," Vaibhavi sighed and put the receiver down on her desk.

She walked up to Arun Sundaram's room and knocked.

"Come in," Arun looked up from the laptop screen, his brow creased.

"Sir, there's a Sonal Verma on the phone who wants an appointment with you. She says it's very urgent."

Arun thought for a few seconds. No, the name did not ring a bell.

"I don't think I've heard that name before. Did she say what it's regarding?" Arun went back to his typing.

"Nothing specific, sir. She said she's from NexGen and that the matter is of utmost importance to her… and, er… to you, sir."

The name 'NexGen' had finally managed to capture Arun's attention. He stopped typing and sat up straight.

"What did you say? She works for NexGen and wants to see me for something that concerns *me*?" Arun checked.

"That's right, sir," Vaibhavi confirmed.

"Okay, I will meet her," Arun paused and then added, "But not in the office. At the Club in the evening tomorrow. At eight."

52

"Sonal Verma, what brings you here?"

Arun Sundaram took a sip of the Corona Extra beer and looked at the girl sitting across the table. They were in Arun's club, sitting by the golf course lined at the horizon by trees that looked like dark blotches of ink against the night sky. The Friday evening crowd in the club was slowly thickening.

Arun was wary of meeting employees from his rival companies in the office, unless it was an unquestionably innocuous scenario, like a job application. Hence, his choice of the venue.

Arun was wondering what the meeting was going to be about. The girl had mentioned just now that she worked in the Administration department of NexGen. She looked very young. Possibly just out of college. Arun wondered how she could be in possession of any information that might help him, as the girl had claimed.

"Mr Sundaram, I have a proposition that will benefit both of us," Sonal cut the chase and came straight to the point.

Sonal's expression did not betray her anxiety. There she was, offering a business proposition to the Head of India Operations of Alpha Tech, while her heartbeats were going berserk.

"Did you say '*us*'?"Arun smiled. He was almost amused.

"Yes."

"I don't think NexGen and Alpha can have any common interest whatsoever," Arun reclined in his seat, stealing a glance at his watch. The meeting was probably going to be a complete waste of his time.

"I'm not representing NexGen's interest here," Sonal bent forward and lowered her voice. "Let's just say that I have a more selfish agenda."

"I see," Arun's eyes hovered over the face of the girl, trying to figure her out. "I hope this is not one of Vikram's dirty tricks. I won't be surprised if I find out later that I was being filmed all this while, striking a deal with a NexGen worker to sabotage one of their business plans," Arun was now feeling apprehensive. Meeting this girl had probably not been such a good idea, after all.

"Mr Sundaram, I would request you to hear me out. You have nothing to lose here, I can assure you. But, we have a lot to gain if we help each other."

Arun gestured to the waiter for another round of drinks. "So, what's your 'selfish agenda'?"

"Let me just tell you that there's nothing that would make me happier than to see Vikram Oberoi lick the dust," Sonal spat out.

"That certainly is a most delightful thought," Arun chuckled. He bent forward and asked, "But how do you propose to make *that* happen?" The condescending smile was still there on his face. The kid had probably been spurned by the hot boss and wanted to get even. Arun was in no mood to get involved in a lovers' tiff on enemy territory.

Sonal went on, "Mr Sundaram, I've been studying the market for a while now and I realize that you are NexGen's biggest competitor at the moment—"

"So, Admin interns at NexGen also do market research when they aren't making hotel and flight reservations," Arun reclined in his seat and laughed out.

Sonal was ticked off. She balled her fists under the table and resisted a retort. "If there's anyone who can destroy NexGen, it's you, Mr Sundaram," Sonal sounded like she meant business, making it amply clear that she was not in the mood to indulge Arun's taunts. "Especially if you have access to classified information. And some luck," Sonal added.

"Access to classified information," Arun repeated. "That sounds interesting to me. What classified information do *you* have access to?"

"Mr Sundaram, this is where I need your help. You need to tell me how we can do maximum damage to Vikram's business. You tell me about those projects where you are competing with NexGen and I will get you everything *you* need to beat the crap out of Vikram in each one of those deals."

Arun looked at Sonal reflectively, his brows creased. "And what's in it for you?"

"I told you, Mr Sundaram. I want to finish off Vikram Oberoi." Arun could see the fire in those beautiful eyes, her face flushed, and her jaws stiff. Something told him that her thirst for retribution was overwhelming. He thought he would ask her why. But he decided against it.

He thought for a while, carefully considering Sonal's proposition. He finally said, "Okay, I'll give this a shot. But, I doubt if *you* know of ways to access 'classified information'. How long have you been working at NexGen?"

"A couple of months. And thanks to my job in the Admin department, I know a lot of Vikram's business associates. I know who he's meeting and where he goes to wine and dine them. I know when and why the bosses are making business trips. Most importantly, Vikram trusts me, and let's just say that he takes more than casual interest in me. For everything I don't know myself, I know of ways to make the right people in NexGen talk." Sonal smirked.

Arun was impressed by the confidence the girl exuded.

"Hmm…" Arun thought for a while, his head bowed. He then said, "But, you'll need to make a lot of people talk, if we want this plan to work. We need to first identify our marks – the ones who're vulnerable and most likely to give in to temptations… money, sex, whatever… if you know what I mean," Arun winked.

Sonal nodded, realizing for the first time the enormity of the task she had set out to accomplish. She said, "I've done my homework, Mr Sundaram. I know our soft targets in NexGen."

"Good," Arun continued while sipping his beer. "But Sonal, you can't do this alone. In fact, I don't want you to expose yourself more than what's necessary. I know of someone who can make the toughest of them go weak in their knees." Arun winked and continued, "Her name is Urvashi, one of the most desirable escorts in town. At least, that's the name I know. She goes by a lot of names. I'll be damned if I know which one is her real name. She's worked for me a couple of times, when I've had to win over clients. She's really good at what she does. I'll give you her number. And I can pick up her bills for you. She can be quite expensive, you know."

After a brief pause, he added conspiratorially, "We need to lay down some rules of the game here, Sonal. We won't meet after today. Don't call me on my official number. I'll give you an unlisted number where we can be in touch. And, Sonal," Arun lowered his voice almost to a whisper and looked her in the eyes, "I hope you realize that you're walking on thin ice here. Don't ever try to act smart with me. I don't easily forgive."

Sonal held his eyes and said, "For me, it's not only about *you*, Mr Sundaram. As I said, I'm here on a mission which will succeed *only* if you are successful, and that's what has brought me here, but it's *my* mission at the end of the day," Arun saw the shadow of malice slide across the girl's face once again.

He leaned back in his chair, and said, "Well then, let's talk business. Have you heard of Evita?"

53

Present Day

Vikram called Sonal's number for the third time after receiving her text, but she did not take his call. When he finally stood up from the sofa, he could barely stand straight. His head felt heavy, his hands and feet numb.

"I've lodged a formal complaint with the police against Mr Vikram Oberoi for his prolonged sexual harassment," Vikram heard Sonal threatening on the television.

Vikram wondered how much time he had before the police landed up at his door.

"You fucking bitch!" Vikram screamed, his words echoing through the empty house.

He looked past the dining area at the bedroom. That was the bed where he had spent days and nights with Sonal. That was the bed where the sex had, over time, turned into lovemaking. His eyes went to the kitchen, where, for the first time ever in all his life, he had made breakfast for a woman. The memories brought tears to his eyes, even as he shivered in rage.

He looked at Sonal on the television one more time. And his lips curled in a wicked smile.

"I'm not going to let you do this to me, bitch! Vikram Oberoi is not going to be dragged away by a bunch of *khakis*," Vikram mumbled as he tottered into the kitchen. He pulled open the drawers of the kitchen cabinet, one by one. He was looking for the knife.

When he finally found it, Vikram felt happy and relieved. That knife was his ticket to freedom.

Wobbling back to the sofa, Vikram poured himself a drink.

"One for the road," he grinned. His eyes fixed on the television, Vikram raised a toast to himself, laughing like a maniac.

"Catch me if you can, bitch!"

He finished the drink in one long swig. He then raised his left hand, the palm facing him. He looked at the lines on his palm. He wondered if his life would have been different, had those lines looked different. It was too late to ponder over those lines. And he was too drunk.

He held the tip of the knife on his forearm. With all his strength, Vikram made a deep vertical gash on his wrist. Laughing hysterically all the time.

He felt a pinch. It then took a second or two for the blood to appear. First, a reddish black line and then the blood started oozing out of his fresh cut.

It seemed as if a weight had been lifted off his chest. He now wanted to paint his wrist more, and he did. Till there was a relentless deluge of blood, warm and thick, that smeared the white leather upholstery of the sofa, and made crimson lines flowing down to the carpet.

Vikram Oberoi had finally made it. The end of a nightmare that would never come back to haunt him.

54

The wind was howling when the police cars stopped in front of Prestige Apartments. The sky was dark, the tall trees surrounding the apartment complex tossed their heads, whispering in the wind, and there was an air of gloom all around.

Vikram Oberoi's private penthouse was on the top-most floor. The police waited for the elevator on the ground floor for a couple of minutes. When they got in, they pressed the key for the twenty-ninth floor. Getting out of the elevator, they walked up to the door of Vikram's penthouse and rung the bell. No one opened the door even after several attempts. Finally, the police broke into the apartment.

The door opened to a living area. A sofa set was spread out in the middle of the hall; with its back to the door. There was a low coffee table in front of the sofa. There were a few magazines on the table. They could see a bottle of whiskey more than half empty. And an empty glass.

There was a news bulletin being aired on the TV, Vikram Oberoi's picture on the screen. A wall clock fixed right above the television showed the time as fifty-five minutes past eight. Adjacent to the main door, there was a bookcase that almost touched the ceiling and was stuffed mostly with fiction and business books. All the windows had their curtains drawn.

At the far end of the room, there was a dining table and a refrigerator. There was a curtain that separated the sitting area from the dining area. That curtain was presently drawn aside. Facing the dining area was a kitchen and beyond the dining area was a door that led to what looked like a bedroom. It was a spacious apartment, just the kind that suited someone like Vikram Oberoi.

The police walked in and stopped in front of the sofa.

Vikram Oberoi was sprawled on it, the sofa smeared with blood, several deep gashes in his wrist being the source. The kitchen knife, its blade coated in his blood, was on the carpet near his feet.

He had long been dead.

"*Tharki saala*," Inspector Salgaonkar smirked. "The bastard ran away to hide inside his hole and called it quits escaping the prison. What an asshole!"

He turned towards his companions. He had *that* look on his face, which his companions knew only too well. Salgaonkar was going to make a philosophical remark. He always made one, when there was a corpse around.

"Look at him. *This* is what happens when you run after money," he paused for effect and continued, "and women."

"Bad example for our kids," quipped another man in uniform.

Epilogue

All the Department Heads at NexGen gathered inside the Conference Room on the twenty-first floor.

The events of the last few days had rattled everyone. Share prices had plummeted, and high-value clients had expressed concern over matters of corporate ethics, no longer certain if they wanted to continue doing business with NexGen. Suddenly, the future of the company and its employees did not look very promising.

Everyone in NexGen, however, had faith in Dev's leadership and his judgement.

So, that morning when Dev summoned all the Department Heads to the Conference Room, the buzz on the floor was that the 'old fox', as he was fondly referred to by some within the company, must have come up with a survival strategy.

When the Department Heads had taken their seats around the table, Dev stood up to speak.

"Gentlemen, these are difficult times for NexGen. Over the last few months, we've been faced with one disaster after another. And I don't want to blame any one person for the mess. It's our failure as a team. It's as much my failure as it was Vikram's. Companies like us set technology trends for the future, but at the end of the day, they are run by human beings, with basic instincts and weaknesses that have defined us since the time we lived in caves.

"In Vikram, I saw an extremely competent professional and entrusted him with the single most important position in the company. But, what I realized over time is that the line between professional excellence and personal integrity is a thin one. The darkness you carry in the hidden chambers of your soul is bound to take in its grasp your conduct at the workplace. And that has got nothing to do with how smart or how learned you are.

"To make its way out of the crisis we are faced with today, this company needs a leader who is not just a visionary, but is someone who has demonstrated exemplary integrity and honesty, not just at work, but also off it.

"And believe me, this is not an impulsive decision. I've been toying with this idea for a while, even before Vikram's tragic demise. And after much deliberation with my business partner Ashok, who unfortunately could not make it to this meeting as he is down with a flu, I have decided to hand over the reins of the India operations of NexGen to Ashwin Saxena."

When Dev paused, there were claps around the table. Ashwin stood up.

"Ashwin, I'm confident that you'll do complete justice to your new position. Ashok also sends his congratulations," Dev smiled warmly.

"I'll try my best not to let you down, Dev," Ashwin sounded confident. He had been waiting for that day for years. He wondered when he would be able to call Ashiya to deliver the news!

He walked up to Dev who shook his hand and hugged him.

"So, what, in your view, should our immediate priority be, Ashwin?" Dev asked.

"Dev, we've got a lot of bad press over the last few days. The clients are shaky. Our stock has hit rock bottom. We badly need a facelift.

"We will go to the media and reiterate our commitment to corporate ethics. With Rakesh Behl resigning from his position as the Head of Advanced Product Engineering, a couple of veteran technology practitioners who are known across the industry are going to join us this week. This will also increase our credibility as a firm, and prove that NexGen is still able to attract the best talent in the market.

"And then, we do what we do best, Dev. Roll out some stunning new products. As quickly as we can. And for that, I'll need everyone's support." Ashwin looked around the room.

"Sounds like a plan, Ashwin!" Dev exclaimed, looking at the Department Heads, who looked reassured and confident. The mood in the room had clearly changed.

"Back to work, boys!" Dev hollered as he headed for the door.

❖

Sonal was in a coffee shop with Urvashi sitting across the table. The two were meeting in person for the first time.

"You know, Sonal, I've never earned more money in any assignment all my life than what I've been paid for this one. Why, you guys even paid for my trip to Tokyo!" Urvashi paused and lowered her voice, "and trust me, one woman to another, that geek I was with in Tokyo was *really* hot! So was Vikram. May his soul rest in peace. Can't say that about the Systems guy, though."

They laughed. And then, Sonal held Urvashi's hand.

"You know, my mission would never have been complete without you," she had tears in her eyes.

Urvashi placed her other hand on Sonal's and said, "You know, I've often wondered why your mission, as you call it, was so important to you. But I never asked. And I won't ask today. But, in all these years, working for an escort agency, I've finally found a reason to feel proud. And that's a gift I'll cherish as long as I live. It matters to me a lot more than all the money I made. Thank you for that." Urvashi's eyes welled up.

Sonal came out of the coffee shop, feeling contented after a long time.

The police and the media now had all the videos Sonal had filmed. She was the new darling of the media, an overnight celebrity. Her story was all over the newspapers and television channels were queueing up for her bytes. But most importantly, she savoured the sweet taste of payback. She was happy that Rishi's death had, at last, been avenged.

Sonal wished Rishi were there to celebrate the moment with her. She turned towards the coffee shop and could almost see

Rishi stepping out in the morning sun, waving at her, running to her and taking her in a hug. She needed a lot of that, now that her battle was over and she suddenly felt exhausted. Sonal was lost in Rishi's arms in her dreams, as the rush hour traffic trudged along the Marine Drive.

❖

Manvi sipped from her cup of green tea as she watched the sun go down into the depths of the Arabian Sea. The world around her had changed dramatically in the last few days. And now, her life unfolded before her eyes like a show-reel of pictures. Some of them pretty, most of them tainted.

The sharp pain from the wound on her soul made her cry all over again. A festering wound that refused to heel, and would probably stay with her for the rest of her life.

It was not about her husband turning out to be an insatiable sex-maniac. It was not about the despicable truth about Vikram's sex-addiction now being laid bare before the world in juicy gossips. It was not about the fact that over the years, Manvi had been reduced to a clog, which Vikram was happy to uproot and throw away to a side as he marched on, in his pursuit of power, wealth and sex. It was not about the farce she had had to put up in front of cameras for years, hiding the scars in her marriage with fake smiles. It was not about the fact that with the name of the family blemished forever, life looked uncertain for her and her little boy.

It was about the sin she had been party to. Silently, shamelessly. Sending her conscience to sleep for months till the media got tired of talking about it. It was about those moments of unpardonable indiscretion inside a hotel room a year back, that she would never forgive herself for.

It was about Rishi Bhargav, a promising young soul, bright and beautiful. A flame she had mercilessly snuffed out in collusion with Vikram, before it could light up the world.

Manvi wondered if she had suffered enough for her sin to be atoned for.

Also by the same author:

Thriller

In the Shadows of Death: A Detective Agni Mitra Thriller

Short stories (Ebooks)

It's All About Love Series:

The Gift

The Cookery Show and a Love Story

A Special Day

Masks

An Autumn Turmoil

The Hunt

The Death Wish

Beyond 22 Yards Series:

Love Beyond 22 Yards

Crime Beyond 22 Yards